Last Stands

Last Stands

Stories by Gordon Weaver

University of Missouri Press   Columbia and London

University of Missouri Press, Columbia, Missouri 65201
Printed and bound in the United States of America
5   4   3   2   1   08   07   06   05   04

Library of Congress Cataloging-in-Publication Data

Weaver, Gordon.
    Last stands : stories / by Gordon Weaver.
       p. cm.
    ISBN 0-8262-1521-1 (alk. paper)
  1. Psychological fiction, American. 2. Life change events—Fiction.
3. Men—Fiction. I. Title.
PS3573.E17L37 2006
813'.54—dc22   2003024711

∞ This paper meets the requirements of the
American National Standard for Permanence of Paper
for Printed Library Materials, Z39.48, 1984.

Designer: Jennifer Cropp
Typesetter: Crane Composition, Inc.
Printer and binder: Thomson-Shore, Inc.
Typefaces: Minion, Esprit, LTZapfino

Publication of this book has been assisted
by the William Peden Memorial Fund.

This one is for Maycee Lynne,

    for the many years to come,

and in memory of Nelson Weaver,

    for the many years past.

Contents

Last Stands

"The stern hand of fate has scourged us to an elevation where we can see the great elevating things . . ."

—David Lloyd George

Looking for the Lost Eden

Once I decide to leave a place, *relocate,* as professional employment agencies say, my perception changes. I become more aware, sensitive to the particulars of the place I'm going to leave. I see more clearly, exactly. This new vision of things is soured by a pessimism, a rejection of this place I'm leaving, yet I'm filled with a positive energy, impatiently eager to get on with the awful drudgery of moving.

No doubt I become a difficult man to live with, adding to the burden already imposed on my wife and daughters by the disorientation of packing and loading our household into a rented U-Haul truck.

My wife, who studied anthropology, makes reference to primitive tribes and religious sects that ritually burn everything they own to cleanse themselves for the turn of each new year. I studied literature, so am put in mind of Faulkner's "Barn Burning," that voice charged with bitter intensity. My wife's expression is softly accepting of the inexorable tedium of our work, while I tend toward sneering and oaths, an energized cynicism.

Here in southern Mississippi, the heat and humidity of late July are intolerably oppressive. Even the early morning sun is too bright, scorching the sky a watery blue-white. The air we breathe pulses with heat, as if it were on the brink of the melting point. The air is thick, like an invisible mist. Each breath I draw tastes warm and wet, tinged with the rankness of the dark green vegetation that seems to grow toward us and the house we're leaving. Now that I'm going, I think of Delta flooding, that we're like croppers gathering possessions to flee before the spreading river engulfs them and their shoddy cabins.

My wife works deliberately, efficiently. I hurry, achieve less in the same period of time, curse the sweat that beads my face, plasters my hair to my scalp, soaks my T-shirt dark in front and back, under my arms. My wife is sensible, pretending the heat doesn't exist. Our daughters are too young to care about such things, to be of any real help in moving.

While we work, they play at the edge of the pine woods. These woods in south Mississippi, I think, now that we're leaving them forever, are alive with cottonmouths and rattlers, armadillos and field mice, snapping turtles and small green lizards, redbugs and poison ivy. I shudder, pray let them be safe just one more day. I feel a deep, sudden guilt for having come here, put my children in such jeopardy, as if I had failed my responsibility as a father. But we're leaving today. With luck and time, I'll soon have them beyond harm.

My helpers, three colleagues I'll no longer share brown-bag lunches and departmental gossip with, two students who will follow other teachers, shout directions to me as I back the U-Haul as close as possible to the porch of the house I've already sold. I've come to be pretty skillful, backing trucks and trailers. I take some pride in it.

My memory of the move my family made from Moline, Illinois, where I was born, to Milwaukee, Wisconsin, stands out from others by virtue of the special, almost electric quality of the epiphany it brought. When we moved, I discovered something fundamental.

My father was a classic case of American upward mobility. His grandfather was an Indiana farmer so poor he went as a hired substitute in the Civil War to pay off his homestead land. My father left home to work in the railroad shops of Hammond, having watched his father struggle with the land around Goshen that only the Amish seemed able to make pay. After a hitch as a flying sergeant at Fort Sill, Oklahoma, and his marriage to my mother, he apprenticed himself to a machinist in a small

Chicago shop. From tool and die making, he rose to detailing blueprints, and from that, with his energy and the application of his natural abilities, he became a design engineer.

From job to better job, through rented apartments and flats in the Chicago area, he led his family at last to Moline, where he headed a department for John Deere, where he bought his first house. The family settled in, his living secure as few others were as the Depression struck and raged. I was born, his late and last child, in 1934.

By 1940, my sister had married and moved to Davenport, Iowa, just across the river. My brother left the next autumn to begin his engineering studies at Purdue. These changes didn't seem to alter my child's world. I'm unable to remember my sister's large wedding or my brother's departure for college.

Of course I didn't know anything about the changes in the larger world that affected our lives. The British Expeditionary Force escaped from the beaches of Dunkirk, France fell to Hitler, and, while Willkie opposed him for a third term, Roosevelt prepared us for war. It opened a great opportunity for my father. He was invited to join an engineering sales firm in Milwaukee. There was going to be another world war. There would be great industrial production for war, and the men who sold this production to the government would be made men.

My memory opens in a kind of aura, a sort of bubble holding the good feelings in which I had always lived. The atmosphere is charged with the anticipation of realizing this marvelous opportunity that has fallen to my father. Everyone is happy. There are rumors of war. There is going to be a great world war, and my father will make his fortune. As my mother goes over the bare floors and baseboards with a dust mop, I think she hums or sings softly to herself. It soothes me like a naptime lullaby. We're going to move to a wonderful new life. My sister is married, has children of her own, lives just across the river in Davenport. My brother's just away, studying to be an engineer like our father, at Purdue University. I'm as happy as only a child wrapped in this aura can be.

I sit on the bare floor—the carpets are rolled and tied, awaiting the mover's van. I have some game or book. My mother has put a housecoat on over her traveling dress to protect it from the dust she raises in this last touch of cleaning. In a corner near the front door, a few cardboard boxes sit, flaps spread open like the wings of large birds, there to receive last things, be packed in the car's trunk just before we leave for Milwaukee. Sunlight gushes at the windows, curtains and drapes already down, stored for this great trip we'll begin today.

Suddenly my father's there—he's been out, making final arrangements. I play on the bare floor, and they talk about me, indulgent, smiling, their joy spilling over and touching me.

My mother says, "You know what he said when I told him today's the day we take our trip? 'I don't want to go. I like it here.'"

"The hell you say," my father says. "The little dickens."

I began to cry. I have never cried harder. No pain has ever been quite like it. I howled, rolled on the floor, didn't hear what they said to comfort me, didn't feel the hands and arms when they picked me up, alarmed. I cried as only a child can cry, unable to feel anything except what made me cry. I don't remember how long I cried, what they did to finally make me stop.

Now, I know what scared me was the realization that nothing in life lasts. The reality of our moving came to me, like a rising warmth becoming hot enough to burn, then sear. It was my first knowledge of change. I understood the transitory nature of existence. In that instant I realized that my sister was gone—married, moved across a wide river to Davenport. My brother had gone away to college, out of our life, someplace called Purdue. The wooden floor on which I sat to play or read, the only home I had known, the foundation of everything, was going— we were leaving it. My father and mother weren't permanent poles defining the axis of my being, only temporary points of focus.

The essence of my existence was conditional, not fixed and solid. If a child of six, nearly seven, can perceive human mortality, that's why I cried and cried.

I always have a dread of beginning, so always delay at the last moment, knowing it's only a delay. "Planning session," I say when the truck is parked, brakes set, doors open, loading ramp in place. "Good work requires we sit down and contemplate the scope here. Besides, we need to get a dent in this beer." The cans of beer have been iced since the night before, the Styrofoam cooler set well back in the deepest shade on the porch. Beer blunts the sting of work when the day gets long, and it'll be hot work.

My colleagues and students sit on sealed cartons while I open and pass out the dripping cans. I'm not dependent on scrounging boxes from liquor stores and supermarkets; for my move from Texas, just four years ago, I bought heavy cartons, folded them flat and stored them away, ready for the next move. They scarcely show any wear.

My wife's a marvelous organizer, has them labeled with Magic Marker so we'll know what can be stowed deep in the truck, what needs special handling to avoid breakage. She comes to the door. "This isn't goofing off," I tell her, "it's a planning session." She knows what has to be done if we're to finish before dark, turns back, irritated, into the house. "First one tastes best," I say, toasting my colleagues and students. But the beer won't really taste good until we've earned it working in this heat. What's important is one last delay.

The way a man dresses for moving day will signify his character. This isn't true of my students, who, in an era of obligatory casual attire, look no different than if we were seated here to conduct a seminar. But it's true of my colleagues, old enough to have evolved the personae with which they most confidently confront experience.

Sonny McCartney, whose area of expertise is modern British fiction (specifically Graham Greene), is a very hard-headed realist. While his usual mode is quite academically correct, suits and matching ties, a vest on occasion, he dresses for this day's work in the oldest serviceable shirt and trousers he owns. The shirt was once a formal pin-stripe with long collar tabs. Faintly comical, the tails hang out and down like a short skirt. Sonny comes from a strong Methodist background in Oklahoma, a life that taught him to see life clearly, what needs to be done, and how, united with a conviction that the only way to do a thing is to do it.

Gary Lee Stringer is, coincidentally, also from Oklahoma, a Baptist preacher's boy, but he's come a further distance from his roots. His dissertation examined erotic elements in Donne's poems, and he teaches that and other Renaissance literature. He's well read in philosophy, knows something of formal logic, is perhaps the best scholar I know. For a day like this, he reverts to a self he long ago deserted.

Wearing greasy mechanic's coveralls, heavy boots, a bandanna around his neck, his speech takes on a nasal twang larded with vulgarities—he is, for this day, the redneck good old boy his intelligence and education refined out of his heritage. He stops short of using snuff or chewing tobacco, though I know he'd be delighted if I had some to offer.

Walter P. Kennedy is a native Mississippian, could have been cast in *Gone With the Wind* if Leslie Howard hadn't been available. What I admire in him is what apologists for the Old South stress, a decorum unflappable in the face of the bleakest prospect. His accent has a honeyed edge in it. He was born and raised less than thirty miles from here, is kin to half this county and the next, wouldn't dream of leaving his native ground. His Levis are brand new, his chambray shirt pressed to a fault.

"Are you still planning or are you ready to get on with it?" my wife comes to the door to ask.

Myself? My shorts are frayed cutoffs, my sneakers worn through the toes, my jersey stenciled with the faded name of another school where I once taught, a spare uniform suited to mobility. I'll drink too much beer this day, clown foolishly like a man twenty years younger. Enough beer, and once I get into the rhythm of this work, absorb its spirit, I'll feel truly young, as if I'm just starting out for the first time.

Off at the edge of our yard, against the backdrop of pines and brush, my daughters play in the shimmering heat. I remember my obligations. "Let's do it," I say, and we begin to load the truck.

My father's new work meant more and more travel. A man who arranged the sale of parts vital to the production of parts in turn vital to the production of still more parts—all of them vital links in the chain of production of things vital to the conduct of the world war—and all this production under guaranteed cost-plus government contracts—had to travel. His employer furnished him a company car, a new 1941 Chrysler, and the government issued him an A sticker for rationed gasoline because he was so vital to the war effort.

He was gone for days, sometimes weeks at a time, crossing and recrossing America's Midwest. Less than two hundred acres of marginal farmland near Goshen, Indiana, purchased with the money his grandfather received as a paid substitute in the Civil War, served as his family's homestead for two generations. My father transcended those boundaries with a vengeance.

My memory of his spectacular success is very limited. His enormous suitcases were laid out on the floor of my parents' bedroom when he was home, never long enough to justify their unpacking. Between trips, he lived out of them just as he did on the road, stopping in hotels in Chicago, Detroit, Minneapolis, St. Louis, and Cleveland.

I would, any number of mornings after getting out of bed, spot the open suitcases in their bedroom, know my father was back late the night before, go downstairs to the kitchen to find him sitting with my mother over coffee while she cooked breakfast, proudly telling her anecdotes of his most recent trip, the latest big deal he had reached with men he once only dreamed of as peers. "I looked him square in the eye," I remember him saying once, "and I told him, I said, 'Look, we've got one swell hell of a war here, let's don't you and me differ to the point of squeezing either of us out of our fair shares, OK?' " I suspect it was as alien a language to my mother as it was to me.

In Milwaukee, before Pearl Harbor, my mother took me to Washington Park to row a boat on the lagoon where black people came to fish for carp. The German-American *Bund* gathered for speeches and picnics there on Sundays. When the war started, the black people still came to fish with their cane poles, but the brown-shirted *Bund* members and their families were gone. When I asked my mother why, she said, "Because they don't permit that nonsense now is why."

I brought money to school each Monday to purchase red war bond stamps to lick and paste into the little booklets that bought one twenty-five-dollar bond when full. Our teachers drilled us in leaving the classroom for damp, dark basement halls when air raid sirens sounded on schedule. There were blackouts at night, and a neighbor came around with a flashlight, wearing a white helmet, to see that our shades were down, curtains tightly drawn. The first naughty language I used in my mother's presence was a song about Mussolini's wienie. My mother saved cooking fat to trade the butcher for meat rationing points, and I learned to help her roll cigarettes with a small machine my father bought on one of his trips, because Lucky Strike green had gone to war.

My sister's husband enlisted in the navy to escape the army's draft. He spent the war in Florida, and never came back. My sister was no doubt mistaken in staying behind for the duration, but she thought the dislocation would be hard on her very young children. She has never left Davenport. Her children grew up, moved away, have children of their own. It's a wonder to me she never left the home she made as a bride. I once asked her why she didn't spend more time visiting her grandchildren. "Every bird," she said, "prefers to stay in its own little nest." She's lived half a century in the same city, on the same block, in that same house.

My brother received a commission when he graduated from Purdue in 1944. I remember when he left. We stood on the sidewalk next to a long bus painted olive drab. My mother hugged and kissed him, and my father gave him some extra traveling money on the moment's impulse, and then my mother kissed him again and said to me, "Kiss your brother good-bye." My brother knelt and hugged me, and I kissed him good-bye.

It's the only time I remember kissing my brother. He was killed, just across the Rhine, in February 1945, is buried in a military cemetery in France. They say the crosses line up perfectly no matter which direction you look. It staggers me to think, now, he's been in France for over forty years. We put a blue star service flag in our front window when he went overseas, then a gold star flag when he was reported killed in action.

My father continued to travel. I remember him telling my mother with great excitement about a flying trip he made to Washington to consult with a Dollar-A-Year man. "What do you think of the old man now, huh?" he said, lifting me. I didn't know what to think. Probably my mother didn't either.

Shortly after my brother's death, my father found a woman who could appreciate what he had become. There were conferences at our dining-room table, my parents and their lawyers haggling over the details of divorce. My father wanted to be very generous, but she wouldn't permit it.

"It wasn't *dastardly*," my father said.

"Yes it was," my mother said. "What else do you call lying and betraying your family? I call it dastardly, and so would your son if he were alive to know it."

I listened. My father shouted, the lawyers reasoned, my mother wept. My father stormed out of the house, slammed the door so hard windows rattled. It felt like the walls trembled, like the house might collapse, as if we had been bombed by the Japs, or the Germans who killed my brother.

The lawyers reasoned my parents through a divorce, and the house, so much newer and larger and finer than the house I had been born in in Moline, was sold as part of the agreement. On the day President Roosevelt died, I stayed home from school to help as much as I could with the packing to move.

With my experience, I should be an expert at loading a truck. I'm competent, but I lack confidence. I suspect I appear lazy when it comes down to the grind of the day's work. It's only that, having made the decision to move, having sold our home, reserved the rental truck, notified the post office, the phone company, and the newspaper delivery boy, having cleared my bank accounts and obtained an auto club map of our route of travel, all with real dispatch, I'm tormented by vague misgivings.

Was this decision wise? Did we get a good price for our house? Will my new position prove all it promises? Will my wife be happy there? Will my daughters adjust quickly, easily, to their new school, find new friends? I hang back, let others seize the initiative.

We begin with heavy appliances, stove, refrigerator, chest freezer, washer and dryer, strap them to the dolly, roll them out, trundle them up the ramp into the truck-bed, which must be heavily front-loaded for proper driving stability. The hierarchy of the crew manifests itself immediately.

Sonny McCartney slaps the side of the refrigerator, designating it the first load. He opens the door to check that trays and shelves will not slide, looks behind it to see the cord will not foul. Gary Lee Stringer rolls in the dolly. I might have guessed.

It's a function of where they come from, identities coherently formed by background, self-concepts so well defined they automatically act out their terms. McCartney, in his clothes—*waste not want not* was surely a family watchword in the country around Duncan, Oklahoma—sees a job of work, begins at the beginning. Stringer, in greasy coveralls, will embrace the worst of the labor, be unfulfilled unless he sweats harder and gets dirtier than the rest of us.

My students are used to subordination. They stand aside to await specific instructions. Walter P. Kennedy, whose chambray shirt will stay unwrinkled all day, though he will not shirk, checks the clearance of door frames, watches for possible obstacles in the dolly's path, keeps a hand on the refrigerator as it wobbles up the ramp. His house, crowded with heirlooms, he knows how to handle furniture without damaging it.

I'm on the fringe of activity, in it but not of it, slowed by a faint paralysis of doubt. Was it wise, this decision to move? Is what I seek to escape so insufferable? Won't I find its like at my destination?

I come up with no answers. I know it's only a kind of bone-deep itch, a chronic irritation of the blood nothing can scratch or stroke. I think of primitive bonfires, of Faulkner's poor white trash. I want to stay. I want to leave. I wish I'd lived here all my life. I wish I'd never seen this place. It's a condition impenetrable to analysis.

After heavy appliances, we string out like safari bearers, loading cartons of books. Books are weighty, make fine ballast to go on and around the appliances. Each move I make, there are more of them. Lifting them, they make me think of an iron collar welded around my neck, Coleridge's albatross. Sometimes, I like to think of their mass increasing to the point where they're transformed into a kind of anchor, fastening me in place for good.

I like to tell my students what a poor student I was. I like to think it humanizes me in their eyes, that it gives hope to those I have no choice but to fail.

The source of my occupation is clear. My grades were so low, my successes so few, reading fiction and poetry was the only world open to me where wholeness and coherence were the norm. I don't confuse fiction with reality—the latter's a series of fragments connected only by time and proximity. The former always yields meaning under study. Reality's a bone I like to chew, but never leads me to anything sustaining.

I had to repeat the seventh grade because I couldn't do the math. My mother conferred with the teacher, and with a psychological counselor from the school superintendent's office. "They say," she told me, "it's because you've been jerked from pillar to post by the shock of your father and I separating."

"What's that mean?" I really wanted to know.

"It means you're having an emotional reaction to your father leaving us you probably aren't even aware of. You can't settle down to concentrate like you should."

I said, "We were barely doing multiplication tables when I started here. I couldn't get long division right off so quick."

"I said you aren't aware of it," my mother said. "You just think it's arithmetic you can't do. It's emotional. They ought to realize that."

"I don't even care anyhow," I said.

"Don't talk like that! Of course you care," my mother said. "Your brother was a brilliant student, and your sister was no slouch." My mother's hopes for me were pinned on her faith in inherited abilities.

After the divorce, my father moved to Minneapolis and married the woman he believed understood what he'd become by virtue of the great opportunity afforded him by the world war. It's a pathetic irony. The war over, the government contracts were canceled. Cost-plus production disappeared until my war came along. My father established his own consulting firm just in time to see his opportunities vanish like smoke in the wind. His second wife divorced him when it was clear he was no longer what the world war made him.

The only time I visited them, in Minneapolis, when I was thirteen or fourteen, they were already on the brink of separating. My father had already decided to move on. "You're old enough to understand these things," he said to me. "She and I'll be going through the wash sooner rather than later. There comes a time when you cut your losses and head for high ground." He moved to Detroit, then to Chicago, then to Long Island, then back to Detroit, where he found a good job as a process engineer. This kept him on the road, to Missouri, to Pennsylvania, back to Long Island, even to Milwaukee once.

My mother moved us often, not because she had to, but because it took her until my war to get over the emotional effects of divorce and my brother's death.

Before the postwar housing shortage eased, we lived in an attic room rented from a Polish family who accepted us as tenants only after my mother promised not to report them for violating the O.P.A. rent guidelines still in law. I remember we ate a lot of boiled eggs cooked on an electric hot plate in the attic room. The Polish landlord complained about this use of electricity, tried to recover his loss by skimping on the heat that record cold winter of 1947. Our soft-boiled eggs smelled of the kielbasa the landlord's wife simmered on the kitchen stove one floor below.

Later, we lived in a series of furnished apartments. All the furniture from our big, new, expensive home was kept in storage until after I returned from Korea in 1954. My professional vita sheet, which I'm scrupulous about keeping updated, shows I attended five grammar schools and three high schools. All my report cards reveal a dismal performance; constant uncertainty is no atmosphere for good work.

When the work of moving gets rhythmic, I embrace it. It's crude—lift, shoulder, join the line of march through the house, keep to the right wall to let others pass me on their way back for another load. Out into the full sun that has begun to ooze across the porch, threatening the iced beer in the cooler. Up the metal ramp that clangs and sways under my shoes, into the darkness of the truck-bed, where Sonny McCartney directs me where to place my carton. This one is labeled *kids winter clothes.*

Where are my daughters? I shield my eyes with my hand, search the opaque liquid shimmer of heat waves for them. Wandered? Lost in the woods? Run away? Gone? I squint, listen, hear their voices, talking with their mother. Safe. Sonny McCartney asks me if I'm declaring a break.

Back and forth, I load my children's clothes and games, I load *fabric* and *extra bedding* and *small utensils* and *glassware fragile.* The moving begins to feel like an end in itself. There's no purpose, no destination, just this work, and it feels right to do it. We pass, all of us, into a silence that further unites us in the routine of tedious work. There's a rhythm now, and rhythm is what gets things done, staying with the job at hand.

I achieve a kind of objectivity. I began to see bare walls and floors of this house the way they looked the day my wife and daughters and I toured the vacant rooms with a real estate saleslady, trying, at her urging, to envision the potential of this space for our family. I'm good at that.

Considering a new home, I see my overstuffed recliner chair in a corner, my wife's desk against a wall, our curtains and drapes blowing gently at the blank windows, where the television should sit. Now, returning these rooms to that pristine emptiness, I lose all memory of how they looked while we lived here. Now, leaving, deep in the steady flow of this work, I can't imagine anyone living here. I can't imagine I ever have, that I ever would. It's a kind of serenity.

This indifference, this pleasant detachment, extends beyond the house as work continues, the day hotter, sun more piercing, air heavier. I marvel at this climate and the landscape. The tall, straight pines in my woods are beautiful, but distant. The vegetation is so lush, so green it looks almost artificial. I search the glossy sheen of the leaves, note hickory, peach, pecan trees, the exotic spikes of palmetto—none of it any more real than they would be planted and tagged in an arboretum. It's as if I'm trying to take what I can with me, as if I'm a visitor with time so short I must concentrate if I'm to recall any of it later.

This work has a way, rhythmically, of becoming everything. I begin to forget I have a past and a future to complicate what I'm doing here today.

I was a pretty good soldier, though I barely qualified as a marksman with the M-1 rifle, while men I trained with were selected for ranger and parachute schools. What I mean is that in wartime a soldier is often in transit, and I was at ease, comfortable, traveling. In basic and advanced infantry training, en route to San Francisco, aboard ship for Japan, at the Eta Jima replacement depot, aboard another ship across the Sea of Japan to the Pusan, Korea, staging area, up the peninsula in a truck to the line perimeter where I was captured by the Chinese Volunteer Army—I remember feeling comfortable, much less concerned than most of the men traveling with me.

I certainly wasn't brave or stoic. I thought about my brother, dead, buried in France for so many years—nearly half my lifetime then—I thought it possible I was going away to be killed, buried forever in a foreign place. I was alert for omens, but found none.

There were no good-byes on the sidewalk outside the Selective Service office. I said good-bye to my mother at our apartment, took a taxi to the Milwaukee Road station, the train to Fort Leonard Wood, Missouri, my ticket paid for with a government voucher. My sister wrote me a long letter from Davenport saying she would pray daily for my safe return. My father, I know, would have sent me money, but he had died suddenly, in Parsons, Kansas, where he'd gone on a consult for his Detroit firm—the marvelous opportunities of cost-plus contract production had returned.

His last letter to me boasted of how much tax-free expense money he received for each day on the road. He'd recently married a fourth wife. I don't judge him, and find solace for his sudden death in the thought that his life ended at a time of great optimism. He's buried there in Kansas, a state he hadn't visited before that last job in Parsons.

I especially liked the long bivouacs at Fort Leonard Wood. There's something deeply pleasing about the compactness of full field gear, the shelter-half that joins another to make an adequate sleeping tent, rolled in the morning and tied to your pack, giving it shape and solidity. Our cadre checked to see we carried the required number of socks and sets of underwear, our apportioned share of tent pegs and C-rations and cartridge clips, each in its own pouch on the web belt. I liked to watch the mess hall and supply and orderly room squads put up their tent flies. The food was good. You broke out mess kits, lined up, were served, ate, washed skillet and tray and cup, packed them away again. I never avoided the work of filling in latrine sumps and loading bulky crew-serve weapons on the trucks. I enjoyed marching, never caring where we were going—it was all predetermined on elaborate training schedules. I could understand why our cadre chose that way of life.

There's an excitement, sitting in the dark on the edge of a group of career noncoms, passing a bottle of whiskey around after a hard day. I listened to them talk about all the places in the world they'd served, other wars, training camps, stories about women, drinking, close escapes, and bizarre combat wounds. I met a sergeant who'd seen the cemetery in France where my brother's buried, and another who wore the Rainbow Division patch on his right shoulder, the World War I Victory Medal on his Ike jacket—he was older than my father. They made the world a large and richly varied place with their talk. They made me want to see it all for myself before I died.

I was never seasick on the troopship, and had the knack of sleeping soundly in what's no more than a limp, narrow trampoline, several decks below topside. I could live out of my duffel bag without any trouble at all. I liked to stand at the rail on the troopdeck and stare at the vista of the rolling ocean, trying to focus on the true horizon through the mist coming up out of the ship's wake in the wind.

We reached Japan, and the men around me began to be depressed or agitated. But Eta Jima was just another smaller Fort Leonard Wood, and the ship to Pusan was just another chance to look at the ocean. Trucks took us north, and then we marched to our assigned perimeter.

I never fired a shot in anger. It was winter, very cold when I woke, zipped snugly into my sleeping bag in a bunker, kicked awake by Chinese Volunteers in quilted coats and tennis shoes. They had overrun us when an ROK battalion on our flank pulled out without telling anyone. I was slapped several times as I dressed, my wallet and wristwatch taken, prodded sharply in the small of my back with the muzzle of a burp gun, but never mistreated after that. The food was awful, and there was never very much of it, but the Chinese were famous for treating prisoners better than the North Koreans did—they even moved us periodically to keep us out of the way of American bombing raids. I never despaired, not a single day up to the day I was repatriated at Panmunjon.

I came away from the experience convinced survival's a matter of psychology. The shock's too great for a few men—I saw some die of it— and it depresses most men. But if you understand, you can live anywhere you happen to be. If you have confidence the situation's only temporary, that a week, a month, a year if the truce talks bog down, will bring freedom, then it's no real trick to endure.

Lunch for my soon-to-be-former colleagues and students goes with the job. My wife calls our daughters in from their play, takes them with her in the family car, returns with white paper sacks stuffed with cheeseburgers, envelopes of french fries, packets of catsup, mustard, salt, and pepper. My daughters are delighted, as if it were a picnic. Don't they realize we're leaving? Would it matter to them if they did understand it? My wife mixes a pitcher of Kool-Aid for the girls, and there's still plenty of beer left.

Sitting on cartons in the last slice of shade left on the porch at this hottest hour of the day, we eat. We've worked long enough to earn this rest, made ravenous by the smell of meat and warm bread as we unwrap the sandwiches. There's only the sounds of paper being wadded, chewing, beer can tabs being popped, drinking, swallowing, sighs. I feel my skin cool a little in the wisps of air that still move now and then. It's like mess call on bivouac, the sensation of rest that's perfect because it separates hard, necessary work into manageable segments, something you can grasp in the mind, discern the ultimate objective, know what you're doing will attain it.

"You're going to be lucky to cram it all in and still get the doors closed," Gary Lee Stringer says, a solid wall of sealed cartons now visible in the dim interior of the truck.

"It'll fit," says Sonny McCartney. "I have it all calculated," tapping the side of his head with his forefinger.

"Don't bet on it," says one of my students. He seems to truly doubt.

"Trust us," I say. "We've been there before. I never believe it can be done when I start, but you always do. You got to have faith."

"If you're going to pull stakes every time you get a wild hair, you shouldn't accumulate so damn much crap," Gary Lee says.

"You mock my worldly good," I say. It strikes me as amusing, so I try to elaborate. "What we have here," I say, standing up, can of beer in hand, turning to my students, playing to them, "What you have here is a tangible chronicle of my very life and times. You see before you all I own. Indeed," I say, since they seem to be listening, "you have carried, all through the hours of this misery, and I hasten to add, will continue to carry until the doors of that U-Haul are padlocked shut for the long trek to follow . . ." I have nothing in mind, trying to make it up as I go.

"Do I have to hear this too, or just them?" Gary Lee Stringer says.

". . . in a sense," I am saying, "you pass my life through your very hands, carry, as it were, something of my being with each box you hump up that ramp . . ." It's not amusing. They stand, stretch, pick up litter.

"Oh, you all will miss us when you're gone," Walter P. Kennedy says.

"Memory," I tell him as we file into the house to resume our labor, "is man's curse, Walter," I say, "laid on man as a penalty for past mistakes." One of my students laughs. I can't tell if he really thinks it's funny.

"Lay off the beer this afternoon," Sonny McCartney says to me.

"I'm serious," I say, and think I am. "It's true. Memory's the curse of the past. The secret way out lies in your vision of the future. The secret's imagining the future. Then the past's no sweat."

"Hogwash," says Gary Lee Stringer.

"*Your* curse is my muscles stiffening up on me tomorrow," Sonny Mc-Cartney says.

"Seriously," I say to my wife, "remember that for me so I can write it down first chance I get." I can't tell if she's amused or not.

I'm pretty effective in interview situations. I express a very genuine enthusiasm for the position—the place, the school, the people—I'm applying to fill. Deans, department chairmen, personnel search and screen committees, they all want to believe a candidate is really serious about joining their community. I am. This is no facade, no role I play for the purpose. I truly feel this desire. I've been eager for every position I've ever held. Naturally, later, I've had some second thoughts.

After a convalescence at Walter Reed Hospital to regain the weight I'd lost as a prisoner of war, I was very anxious to take my accumulated pay, exercise my vet's benefits, and go to college. I suppose I must have chosen Purdue out of some response to the memory of my dead brother. Maybe Indiana still existed for me as the place of my father's origin, and, hence, ultimately, my own? I can't imagine what I might have hoped to find. I began as an engineering major, but soon fell against the hard rocks of precision and finitude. I switched to literature as a sophomore.

I went to Iowa for my master's program. There, I met and married my wife, who was willing to give up her graduate work in anthropology to go to Ohio with me, where I earned my doctorate with a dissertation treating some aspects of American frontier culture in selected novels. Few of my professional colleagues share my interest in Natty Bumppo.

My first position was at a small liberal arts college in Boston. Those days, before the tight market that now makes mobility very difficult in academia, you could find openings in the region of your choice. It seemed ideal to me to begin my career where the Transcendentalists laid the intellectual foundations of our civilization.

We stayed only two years. The Northeast megalopolis soon began to feel tired, enervated, shabby. Maybe we sensed the coming urban crisis, and didn't want to begin a family where we wouldn't like to see our children raised. Maybe it was just that the accent John Kennedy made fashionable offended my midwestern ear.

I taught for three years at another small college in western Pennsylvania, but salary increases were too small to hold me there. Our first daughter was born, and I found what looked like an excellent chance for professional advancement almost all the way across the continent, in Utah.

My wife and I sometimes find ourselves thinking of that trip west at the same time—towing our car behind the U-Haul. We remember it at the same moment, in the same light. It's our archetype, against which we measure and define all other moves. We remember it as open stretches of pasture and rangeland, dry heat, tepid wind coming in the truck's windows, our small daughter very uncomfortable and unpleasant between us on the seat of the cab, the drone of the engine held constant by its governor at forty-five miles per hour. I've had dreams about that highway, spinning out ahead and behind us, like it had no beginning, no end.

Utah seemed a fine place. Our second daughter was born, and my job went well. I began, as they say, to make a small mark or two in my profession.

Then came a series of changes in the higher administration. Promises that had recruited me were not kept. Politicians began to meddle, prompted by newspaper headlines reporting campus unrest in distant places. I didn't decide to leave until after I was granted tenure. Tenure's supposed to guarantee a professor's academic freedom, but it felt to me like a door closing, a cage built to commit me until mandatory retirement in a place I had no reason to love, in a landscape as alien as the moon's.

We left, first for Arizona, then Texas, then Mississippi.

Each new place, new school, has been an objective I've actively sought, something more interesting than the one before. I never, in interviews, condemn the people or places I've left behind. I find a sympathetic ear more often than not. People seem to understand that everything's complex. The forces that move us are likely to be larger than any individual can totally comprehend.

This time, we're on our way to Oregon, a state I've never seen.

I think I know how pioneers on the American frontier felt. It's a wonder to me, the wagons they traveled in, the hardships and dangers they faced, how slowly they went behind yoked oxen. It almost shames me, with my U-Haul truck, my wife and daughters following behind to make a caravan, the four-lane highways mapped out in advance by the auto club, motels with color television, swimming pools, air conditioning, ice-cube machines, waiting for us at the end of each day. Still, there's an important fundamental analogy.

It hits me when the work's finished. It's no cooler, but the sun's below the horizon, the dusk deepening so gradually, yet so swiftly. We turn on all the lights in the house for a last tour and check, then turn them off, and it's suddenly so dark. I operate more by touch than sight as I close the doors on the back of the truck, throw the hasp in place, snap the lock shut.

My wife and daughters arrange the interior of the car for the short trip to the local motel where we'll wash off the day's grime, get a good night's sleep and an early start in the first light of the new day. I watch my wife and daughters. How do they feel about this? Are they only tired, or is there a sadness at leaving that lies behind their weary expressions? Don't they feel any anticipation?

My former colleagues and ex-students sip their last cans of beer on the porch, darker shapes now against the darkening sky. "Take the rest with you," I say to my students, and slip them money, as if it was them going somewhere, on a long journey.

"Go home," I say to my former colleagues, "before your wives start thinking you took off with us." My wife comes to say good-bye, reminds them to tell their wives to write her, she will be sure to write them. I shake hands all around. I feel no sadness, not a shred of sentiment at this parting.

I'll miss them later, but not now, and not for very long, I think. "Keep in touch," is all I say. Walter P. Kennedy hugs my wife's neck, as they say in Mississippi. Their cars pull out, taillights winking shut over the first rise in the land. I'm already forgetting them.

"I'll follow you to the motel," I say to my wife. I'm impatient, wish we could start from here, drive through the night, hit the dawn rising up from some horizon we've never seen before. I think this is how the pioneers felt. An energy comes, flooding away everything else. I climb into the cab of the truck, feel strong, alert, fresh. I could drive for days without sleep.

"I'm so tired," my wife says as she leads our daughters to the car, and, over her shoulder to me, "I hope this isn't a mistake."

"Think positive!" I say, starting the truck's engine. "Think positive!" I call after her. "Besides, if we don't like it we can always pick up and leave, right?" But she can't hear now.

I follow her out the drive. She tops the rise, disappears for an instant. I give the truck gas to hit the incline with good speed. For a second the headlights lose themselves in the air, as if I drove in total darkness, out of, into darkness. I floor the accelerator, want desperately to reach the top, cross it, catch my wife and daughters. For just a moment, in this illusion of darkness, it's as if I've lost them, must hurry, catch them, take them with me, safe, into our future.

A Dialogue

It was still pitch dark out. Mikey stood waiting with his hands in his pockets, jacket collar up against the misty wind that fluttered his hair. When Gruber finally pulled up, he stood there until Gruber leaned over and opened the passenger door for him. He got in and put the briefcase between his feet on the floor. The seatbelt buzzer came on when Gruber put the car in drive.

"You're not buckling up?" he said.

"Hell with it," Mikey said. The buzzer stopped buzzing.

"You're the one in the death seat," Gruber said. He pulled carefully into the freeway's light stream of very early commuter traffic, then across into the passing lane.

"Big joke," Mikey said.

"Oh ho!" Gruber said, and laughed. "He's in a fine mood this fine early morning, isn't he, Mikey boy," he said.

Mikey said nothing, then, "Crapping weather," looking out the window at the roadside and the pavement stained with the wind's mist and the near total dark. "Crapola," he said, not to Gruber, but as if he spoke a purely private thought aloud.

"I think we got up on the wrong side of bed this morning," Gruber said.

"Will you lay off me?" Mikey said. Then they drove without speaking for several minutes. The mist in the wind thickened, became a light rain, and Gruber switched on the windshield wipers. They said nothing, the only sounds in the car the sticky sound of the tires on the wet concrete and the rubbery rasp of the wiper blades, melded in the efficient hum of the car's engine.

Gruber shifted in the safety harness from time to time. He suffered hemorrhoids. He had an inflated pad he sat on when he drove his own car. Mikey found the rental's ashtray and smoked two cigarettes before Gruber rolled his window down an inch for ventilation.

"There's an air vent switch somewhere if you just look for it," Mikey said.

"Give me the fresh air," Gruber said. He wiped at his cheek with the heel of his hand when spatters of rain came in the open window. When Mikey lit another cigarette, Gruber said, "Those things'll kill you, son."

"Tell me some news," Mikey said, and, "Hell with it all," and, "It's my funeral." They were silent again for a moment. Then Mikey put his cigarette out and said, "You could just say a word once in a while, Gruber, if it wouldn't break your back, I mean."

Gruber took his eyes off the road to smile at him as he spoke. "Now whatever in the world made me think you weren't interested in chit-chat this fine morning."

"OK. Smart off," Mikey said. He folded his arms across his chest, took a deep breath.

Gruber said, "I'm sorry. OK? I said I was sorry. I'm driving or I'd get on my knees. OK?"

"OK."

Gruber took his right hand from the steering wheel, made a fist and mock-punched Mikey in the arm. "OK," he said. "Now there's me fine Mikey boy I knew was back inside there somewhere." He put his hand back on the wheel. He was smiling, but kept his eyes on his driving.

"I suppose you never had a day you'd just as soon hang it all up," Mikey said.

"No," Gruber said, "Sure not. I just got this old on nothing but roses since day one." Gruber was fifty-six years old. The fact surprised him when he thought of it. He didn't usually *feel* fifty-six. He felt it, felt his hemorrhoids and sciatica, tired easily on long days that had never fazed him when he was a young buck. Usually he didn't *believe* he was that old, no longer a young man, but accepted the fact of it. Facing a long day like today, he felt old because just the thought of a long day tired him, knowing he would be dead-tired when it was over.

"OK," Mikey said. "Wise old man of the hills. So where's your wiseness? I guess you got all the answers, huh?" Mikey was just thirty. Gruber thought about that, that he had been twenty-six the day Mikey was born, all that life before, since, while Mikey was just a baby, a kid, a snot punk. He didn't smile. The thought made him feel very old. He felt his joint aches, the bulge of his flabby abdomen, his bad teeth, the look of his face, lines, bags under his eyes, the worn look of himself in the mirror staring back at him early this morning. He felt jealous that Mikey was so young, that he, Gruber, was getting old, was old.

"You know me long enough to know I never butt in anything personally," he said.

"Oh yeah," Mikey said, and, "How old are you, actually, Gruber?"

Gruber made himself turn and smile a wide smile. "Fifth amendment," he said. "Those who say don't know. Those who know ain't saying," he said, and then, "How old you think I am?"

"Fifty-six, seven?" When Gruber laughed loudly, Mikey said, "I don't make my living guessing ages in the carnival, you know."

"You're close enough," Gruber said.

"How long you been married? I'm serious, OK?" Gruber looked at him a moment, believed he was serious, decided it was something he should do, talk seriously with him.

"Thirty-one years some-odd months."

"Really?"

"Really. You can check it out."

"Zowie," Mikey said. "I thought I'm married eight and a half years was long."

"It's longish," Gruber said. "Hell, see, you were hitched before I was. What, twenty-two?"

"Twenty-one. My wife was only seventeen, you know. What the hell's anybody know then."

"Nobody knows so all fired much no matter what age they are," Gruber said.

"What's the hardest part for you??"

"Pick a spot," Gruber said, then, "I'm kidding. Seriously, you having wife troubles? Remember I said I don't like being a buttinsky. You brought it up."

"Not what you're thinking," Mikey said. "I wouldn't even call it my wife at all. Everything and nothing," he said. He did have words with his wife this morning, but there was no serious trouble in his marriage. His wife had loved him since the day she met him, and Mikey loved her. They had a son, nearly seven now, and a baby daughter. Mikey loved his family, and they loved him. It wasn't his marriage, however angry he'd been so early this morning when she complained of how he'd be gone, she'd be stuck in the house with the kids from practically the middle of the night until he got back God-knows-when, harping it wasn't her fault they overslept and he had to rush like hell to meet Gruber.

The truth was Mikey had so much going for him, yet could not shake the despair gripping him so often from the moment he woke mornings.

Gruber clucked his tongue, shook his head, smiled. "Mikey me boy, five minutes reflection'll convince you you got it made in the shade."

"Big joke."

"Will you listen to the wise old man?" Gruber said. "If I'm so old and gray then I've been down your road some, right? OK. From where I sit," he said, easing himself in the harness, "you're looking pretty good, boy."

"Sure. Stroke me, I'll shut up," Mikey said. He said it humorously, because he wanted to be told how good things looked for him from Gruber's viewpoint; he knew it looked good for him, believed it, thought someone else's saying it would make it more real, solid, something he could hold on to whenever he felt lousy about things. They laughed together.

"Oh, Mikey! Mikey, Mikey. Consider. Thirty years old. You have the best yet to come, son. Don't tell me you'd like to be twenty-one again."

"I'll grant you that one," Mikey said.

"Nor would I be thirty. And you think thirty's a big birthday? Forty's worse. Wait a few, Grampa Gruber'll tell what's it all about at sixty."

"OK, OK."

"I'm dead serious, Mikey. Take for example your lovely wife. The only one I wouldn't trade for her's my own. I mean that as a very sincere compliment to you, and to her, Mikey."

After a moment, Mikey said, "I appreciate that."

"Your wife and family, you have beautiful children, Mikey," Gruber said. "So, *so* important. You have a treasure no one can take away from you." Gruber spoke very sincerely. He and his wife had had difficult early years together. When their older daughter was a toddler, they had separated for several months. He'd behaved very ugly in all of it. It made him shudder inwardly to think now how close he came to losing his family once. He smiled.

He'd sowed his oats, then gone back to her, begged, *begged* her to try again with him. It worked. They had another child, second daughter, the secret symbol of their marriage's salvation, resurrection. The wonder and joy of it rushed through him as he drove the rental car on the freeway. He had to concentrate on the road, the centerline, traffic, the median, tighten his fingers on the wheel to keep tears from starting in his eyes.

"Never forget to count your blessings, Mikey."

"I don't."

"Of *course* things go to hell on you every so often. It wouldn't be life if it didn't. Always count your blessings, Mikey. And also you've just got to tough it out by your lonesome on occasion too."

"I can be as tough as I need to be," Mikey said. He meant that, how tough he was, could be, and he believed that. It was as if he'd just remembered a basic fact of life. He felt much better. He thought how much he liked Gruber, wished he could say just how much, directly, tell him. Instead he looked out the window at the first glow of dawn.

"Also recognize what's beyond your power," Gruber said. He was thinking of his older daughter's bad marriage to a pure and simple son of a bitch who gave her four years of misery before Gruber stepped in and put a stop to *that*. She lived nearby, with *her* two daughters, grandchildren so beautiful they made Gruber and his wife all but cry when they talked about them. Of course his daughter wasn't grateful to him for what he'd done, but some things were beyond his power. His baby—

he laughed to think he called his second child a *baby*—had graduated college, married a college sweetheart, lived far away, but was very happy. He had to resist tears again.

"What's funny?" Mikey said.

"Nothing. You coming on with the weight of the world on your shoulders. I don't mean that sarcastically. Just that everyone carries his own problems. My cautious opinion is you're man enough to carry yours, so cheer up, Mikey me boy-o."

"It's nothing specific," Mikey said. Suddenly his despair came back to him, stronger than ever. For a second he thought he would swear or smack the dashboard with his fist, unable for an instant to find any words. "Talk about the world!" he said loudly. "I don't know. So maybe it's just I'm some big jerk. I get restless. A person has certain ambitions, too, you know." Gruber nodded.

"Mikey's ambitious!" he said, leaning over to slap Mikey's knee.

"That's a crime?" He narrowed his eyes and looked at Gruber until the older man took his eyes off the road, smiled at him and laughed. "I'm serious here," Mikey said.

"Of course it's not. It's what made this country great," Gruber said, and laughed again. "Forgive an old-timer, Mikey. From over here you don't have any complaints coming on that score either. Or are there things I don't know?"

Mikey's anger evaporated. He truly liked and admired Gruber. He thought hard before he spoke. "I'm not sure I can put it in words." Gruber nodded. "Maybe it's just me."

"Maybe," Gruber said.

"OK, I'm thirty years old. Sure, that's young compared to you. Don't laugh. I don't mean it smart-aleck or insulting. I really need to figure it out."

Gruber stopped laughing. "You've got my undivided attention," he said, and, "At least for a while yet." He looked at his wristwatch, checked it against the dashboard clock. It was almost light out now.

"There's time," Mikey said, and was quiet a moment, checked his own watch, then tried to say what was on his mind. He looked straight ahead as he spoke, as if it were him driving instead of Gruber. He needed to concentrate to make it as clear as he could, for himself, even if Gruber couldn't understand. He didn't want Gruber to distract him, afraid he'd feel foolish or get angry if Gruber laughed.

"It's sort of like trying to think about something as vague as time," Mikey said, looking again at the rental's clock. "Ever think about time passing and all? You can't nail it down tight like you can a job you're doing. You call it ambitious. Like I want to be some big wheeler or something. Don't laugh, OK? OK, I want to get ahead in life. That's a crime? Everybody does. You do, or if you don't you'll admit you did when you were my age, right?" He looked at Gruber.

"I'll fess up to that, Mikey. And, no, there's nothing the matter with wanting to get ahead of the game. All I can tell you is life's got disappointments in store for you, no matter how well you do."

"I'm not getting personal when I say things," Mikey said. He was very embarrassed. He was where he was at age thirty. Gruber was where he was at probably age sixty almost, where he'd be until he packed it in. Mikey's ambition felt mean and jealous to him. He wished he'd said nothing, swallowed his mood and gotten on with the day's work.

"I take no offense. I'm not sensitive that way, Mikey." He looked at Mikey, smiled to show he meant it. He *did* mean it! He could recall the feel of ambition, frustration, whatever it was under the younger man's skin this morning. He tried to bring back that faint but total itch, remembered it associated with the bad time of his life, when he'd separated from his wife, almost lost what proved to be the treasures of his life, wife and children and grandchildren.

"Mikey," he said, "I'm not sensitive, and I do understand you, what you're saying. I'm a realist, you know," he said. "I've come to middle age, and I know who I am. And I think I know the score pretty well. And I accept things the way they are, what life itself is. I can tell you this, but probably you have to learn it all for yourself. We all take our personal lumps. If we're smart, not jerks, we learn to live and accept."

It struck him that what he was saying was very wise, was everything he'd learned by experience, being alive. He wanted to smile, laugh hard at himself, because he knew it sounded empty to the younger man. There was no way to put it into words. He had to be who he was; Mikey could only be Mikey. He, Gruber, could only listen, talk like this, wish his young friend well in life from the bottom of his heart.

"I don't know what anything *means,*" Mikey said. He heard his voice sounding like he wanted to cry. He blinked, swallowed hard before he continued. "I can look at any one thing and see I got no reason to kick." He tallied his good fortune, how everything was going so well for him, on the fingers of one hand with the index finger of the other. "My wife and kids. Money. I got no kicks on money. I know I'm doing good. And no matter what anyone else thinks about it, I see myself being on the way up. I'm not comparing with you, but I honestly don't believe I'll be where you are when I'm your age. I'm sorry if that sounds like a crack. I got excellent health. I got no bad vices. If I quit smoking I'm the cleanest liver you know. I hardly ever take a drink. You know me."

"I think I do, Mikey," Gruber said.

"So what the hell's wrong with me then?" He held his hands out, palms up, closed his eyes.

"Not a thing," Gruber said. And, "I'll say this once, short and sweet. Believe it or not, it's up to you. Know what your trouble is? Mikey, you're only human. It's what life, living, is, boy! It proves you're alive at least. You wouldn't be the person I know if you didn't get this way now and again. Accept. It's like time. Where's it start? Where's it end? We're not philosophers, and we're not priests. Who has any answers? People felt this way long before we were knocking around, and it's all going to keep on after we're gone. In the humble opinion of yours truly. Am I making sense to you? So write me off, I'm just another old jerk shooting off his bazoo."

"No," Mikey said. "No, I understand what you're saying. You're right," he said, "but it still doesn't make a whole lot of sense in the end, does it."

"Thinking about it," Gruber said, "where does it get you? You like ulcers? Nobody asked to be born. Personally, I'd a whole lot rather be than not be. So would you I think."

"OK," Mikey said. They sat in silence, and Mikey examined himself to see what he thought and felt. His feeling of despair lessened. He ticked off in his mind the many good things in his life, and they were all there and real. But there was still a kind of gray, vacant feeling behind it all, inside him, not good, not bad. Like the weather today, rain slacking off again to a blowing mist, sky still overcast but much lighter now, the sun coming on back there somewhere.

He lit a cigarette, thinking how much he enjoyed smoking. But he'd break that habit one day soon, put his mind to it, a decision, mark a date on the calendar, tough it out. That made him feel a lot better, that he knew he could focus on something to do, do it, be better for it. That made sense. He enjoyed his cigarette.

"Here we go, Mikey," Gruber said. It was fully light now. He checked the rearview and side mirrors, made the long gradual turn with the increased traffic into the cloverleaf exit. Gruber couldn't help smiling a little to himself. He thought of himself as a man who took days as they came. He'd known some bad ones, more good ones. The weather was clearing up ahead. He was very comfortable behind the wheel. This was a pretty good day. Good for him, better for Mikey than it started out. He had done that, made it that way, listening, talking seriously, taking the younger man seriously. He was pushing sixty, but he didn't feel it.

"Let's earn it," he said.

There were several blocks to drive, a strip of fast-food places, gas stations, carpet showrooms, automobile dealerships, before they took up their position in the still empty small shopping mall. Mikey opened the briefcase between his feet, removed the pistols and the silencers, laid one pair on the seat between them while he fitted the silencer to the barrel of the other pistol. He handed it to Gruber, who laid it carefully in his lap. Then Mikey fitted the silencer on the second pistol and held it with both hands in front of him, the muzzle of the silencer pointed up to the roof of the car.

They sat in the mall's parking lot, waited. The first car that came in after them parked, but a woman got out, walked to a boutique, unlocked and entered.

"Bingo," Mikey said when the next car pulled in. A man got out, started across the lot toward a pharmacy at the far end of the mall. They got out of their rental car and walked after him. They walked fast, all but trotting. The rain had stopped, but the air was very damp. Their shoes made a slapping echo as they hit the mall sidewalk and closed on the man.

The man saw them when he stopped at the pharmacy's entrance, digging beneath his topcoat for his keys to open the door. He saw them, but thought nothing of them until Mikey jumped off the sidewalk, onto the asphalt, to cut the man off if he tried to run. Gruber walked up to within six feet of the man.

The man looked at Gruber, then half-turned to look at Mikey, who stopped at the curb. Mikey pointed with his pistol at the man. The man turned back to Gruber, and saw Gruber's pistol pointed at him. His hand was still in his pocket, his other hand holding his coattail, lifting it to make it easier to get his keys. His mouth was open, as if he meant to speak.

Gruber shot him three times in the chest. The pistol twitched in his hand as it went off. The silencer made a loud, abrupt whistling sound. The man was thrown backward into the pharmacy entranceway, where he collapsed, head against the wet tiles.

Gruber put his pistol down at his side. Mikey stepped up on the side-walk, crouched, aimed with both hands and shot the man in the side of the head. He stepped back after he fired, held his pistol out and away from his body, looked down at the front of his jacket to see if he had been splattered. Then they both watched the man closely to see if he was still alive. There was a sound of rainwater dripping from the mall's eaves. Then Gruber gave his pistol to Mikey and they walked quickly back to their car.

They said nothing until they were back on the freeway. Mikey re-moved the silencers from the pistols, packed pistols and silencers back into the briefcase between his feet. Then he lit a cigarette and said, "How old would you guess him for? I'd guess forty."

"Forty, forty-five," Gruber said. He squirmed to find a comfortable position on the seat for his hemorrhoids.

"Dumb jerk," Mikey said.

"Now that's not our call to make, is it," Gruber said. Mikey shrugged and watched the smoke curling up from his cigarette.

"He should of stayed in bed," Mikey said. He laughed, but Gruber did not. It began to rain again, and Gruber switched on the windshield wipers, switched off the headlights because it was full day now.

The White Elephant

It had a history. It was built by a childless Greek couple with their life savings in 1930. The Greek wished to settle back and run a neighborhood grocery during the last third of his life, and his wife never opposed his plans. He had it built well, with extra-heavy floor joists and studding, and walls of expensive, finished brick.

From the beginning, it was painted white. A back door opened on the yard of a padlock and chain factory. The front door was in the exact center of the facade, and on either side of the door were large display windows. By the time the Greek opened for business in 1931, dressed in a white paper hat and clean apron, prepared to do his own butchering, he was already apprehensive about the constant public reassurances that the Depression was only temporary.

Despite the calm statements of the Hoover administration, the Depression clasped its soft dark hands around the eyes and ears of the nation, seeming to squat directly on the working-class neighborhood where the Greek had dreamed of selling fresh meat, vegetables, and canned goods. Instead of the cheerful daily singing of his secondhand National cash register, humanized by the gossip of regular customers, he knew the drag of long, gloomy days, his temples between his palms.

31

He listened to the hidden rafters creak. The windows rattled when trolley cars passed on the street outside. He could not bear to look at his wife sitting in a chair at the rear of the store, watching the front door. Her expression was taut, drawn. She might have been expecting the devil himself to enter, the line of her anxious mouth breaking occasionally, as if she sometimes feared even the devil would pass their store by.

When the bell over the door rang, it was only to signal a little girl fetching a dime's worth of hamburger (three patties), or a man carrying a bucket, soap, and rags, asking if the Greek wanted his display windows washed cheap, or a band of boys hauling shopping bags clinking with soda bottles they'd scoured the area for, wanting the deposit to take and spend elsewhere for candy.

The first snow in 1932 fell sluggishly, the sky gray and thick with an insidious, damp cold. The Greek looked up to see a housewife tromp by through the slush, stop in front of his store to stamp her shoes clean in the space he'd shoveled before his door, look in hastily, then move on, a net shopping bag hanging out of her purse. It was anticlimactic; there had been no question of the finite, inexorable end for several months. The Greek rose from his stool behind the counter.

Tearing his hands from the sides of his head as though he meant to pull his ears off, he stood in a pose of crucifixion for a moment. The pencil behind his left ear clattered atop the dry goods and notions case. He brought his palms down on the bare countertop, and his wife popped up and down once on her chair at the noise, her fingertips flying to her mouth. "Ah!" she said, as if the devil *had* entered, invisibly, and secretly possessed her husband.

The Greek looked at her as he swept his light Toledo scales onto the floor. "My life!" he shouted at her. "My life!" when she did not respond, understand at once what he had just perceived. "The whole thing," he snarled, and running from behind the counter, worked out his rage.

Seeing what he had built with the savings of two-thirds of a lifetime—his building, a stone hung around his neck—and that he could not scramble madly enough, could not tread water fast enough to keep from drowning under it—certainly he deserved his moment of ranting.

"My life, my damn life!" he said, but did not swear because he was always unsure of his English. He seized handfuls of potatoes from a bin, pelted the walls. An open bushel basket of lightbulbs was spilled on the floor, exploded beneath his shoes. He hopped one-footed along the front of his store, kicking savagely with his free leg at the bottom of the window display platform, the door, tinkling the little bell, then the other display platform. Slamming sideways into the shelves of canned goods, their tops no longer devotionally, hopefully, and hopelessly dusted each day by his wife, he winced, turned, screamed once more, "My life!" to his wife, who backed into her corner, tiny tears running over her cheeks; he charged his meat, poultry, and dairy case.

When the cold double glass would not shatter under his fists, he collapsed there against it and wept for a protracted period of time.

He was not alone. Powerful speculators inserted revolver barrels in their mouths, stoically pulling the triggers as stock tickers chanted progressive ruin into silent rooms. Unemployed men drank courage sufficient to slash their wrists or leap into rivers or commit crimes. A famous man in the city had hung himself by his own suspenders (in his bathroom) only the week before.

But not the Greek. His wife left her corner, held his aching head in her arms and talked swiftly, soothingly, to him in Greek. He composed himself, dried his eyes on his spotless apron, and soon after, went into legal bankruptcy. With Greek courage, he finished his life in the normal course of time, in bondage to a brother-in-law, driving one of a fleet of three coal trucks.

In the liquidation of his assets the property was acquired by a shrewd man named Israel Myer, who had gotten his start before the stock crash, selling nonexistent pre-need burial plots that were actually on the bottoms of several of the ten thousand lakes of Minnesota. He spent the year 1930 in the Illinois state prison at Joliet, emerging shrewder than ever. The promise of Repeal in 1933 prompted him to buy the Greek's lot and building out of receivership. He leased it to a man from Chicago who had speakeasy experience. At the precise moment of Prohibition's death, the building, drastically remodeled, came to life again, this time as a neighborhood tavern. The Chicago lessee failed after two years.

The Depression had not ended; the bitter spirit of the Greek seemed to haunt the structure. When the first lessee failed, Israel Myer simply found another, for the city was filled with men willing to bet on themselves and FDR. It continued to fail. Between 1933 and 1958, the former grocery store was known, in order of sequence of financial failure, as The Cozy Corner, Nub's and Nina's, The Tuxedo, The Elbow Room, Betty and Dad's, Squeeze Inn, and Chet's.

Tavern trade was very good after the war began, but by 1941 the tradition of doom was strong in the Greek's building. The Elbow Room managed to survive through the war, knowing brief moments of ephemeral solvency by serving underage sailors and installing slot machines. The sailors evaporated with the atomic bomb dropped on Hiroshima, and police activity eventually materialized. A John Doe investigation of creeping municipal vice was under way in the city. The slot machines were confiscated and destroyed with axes and sledges in the basement of the Public Safety Building after a surprise raid. A photo of the destruction was printed in the local Hearst paper.

When Chet died of a stroke in 1950, his widow was destitute. Israel Myer, stalking bigger game this time, did not release the property. The building had aged. The white brick walls were a uniform dingy gray. The three steps from the sidewalk to the doorsill were rotted beyond repair. One window cracked in a storm, and was held together now with patching rivets and washers. The plumbing did not always function. Rats from the city's sewage system infiltrated the basement.

It became a corpse of a building. Transients took to breaking in to sleep or drink their lonely wine. The remaining furnishings were stolen or destroyed by teenage vandals. Twice between 1950 and his death, Israel Myer engaged lawyers to oppose court orders to show cause why he should not be held in contempt of the city's sanitation ordinances. There was growing public concern about infectious urban blight at the time.

It was a liability on the books that Israel Myer Jr., a millionaire by virtue of his father's death, inherited in 1957. The son had already shown a determination to create assets from nothing more than his own pure energy and ambition if need be.

This is how Ray Neery came to manage the new tavern business in the Greek's building at an important juncture in his life, when he was thirty years old.

He was hand-picked by Myer Jr., who understood that business is a

function of personalities. The millionaire looked about and saw Ray
Neery, who except for some part-time work as a bartender had never
been anything other than an air spade operator on tunnel construction
projects until recently, when he had been promoted to tending the decompression chamber because his father was crew foreman. In the decompression chamber, Ray read books of politics, history, and science
fiction between the hours when the sand hogs changing shifts sat and
talked with him above the hissing of the chamber. But because he
sought a personality, there were other factors considered by Myer Jr.

Ray Neery was treasurer of the county Democratic Committee, and
Myer Jr., a conspicuous liberal since college days, was its chairman. Ray
Neery had run for office in his local of the Hod Carriers & Common
Laborers Union and been only narrowly defeated by the entrenched in-
cumbent. A minor hero in Korea (Bronze Star with V for valor, Purple
Heart), he would certainly be commander, soon, of his American Legion
post. Ray's parents (he was the oldest of seven children) had lived in the
neighborhood ever since their marriage. In his youth, Ray Neery had been
the acknowledged leader of a modestly delinquent gang headquartered in
Steuben Park.

Ray was well known, and Myer Jr., his only remaining obstacle the
upstate old guard Democrats who dominated rural delegations, was
planning on running for governor in 1960.

"It's business, Ray," Myer Jr. said, "but it's more than that too." A
modern millionaire, he kept his collar open, maintained a plain office,
and did not bother to have his law degree framed and hung. He employed lawyers when he needed them, never having been admitted to
the state bar to practice after his graduation from law school. "I'm investing in a property, but more important, I'm investing in you. It's your
job and future; I'm just the money. On the other hand, let's face it, I'm
willing to send a dollar out on the rounds, and another one to go look
for the first one if I have to. But I expect them to come back. And bring
friends along with them." He kept cigars on his desk, but no one had
smoked one in his office since his father's death.

"I just want you to know how serious I'm taking this, and how much
I appreciate the break you're giving me, Ike. I know I'll never get a break
like this again. Believe me, I'll give it everything I've got," Ray said. He

refrained from visibly swallowing too often, was conscious of his dislike of ties and white shirts because he had worn them especially for this meeting, and checked his fingernails often throughout the conversation to reassure himself he had scraped them clean with his pocketknife blade. He was pleased he could call a proven millionaire *Ike* to his face, yet uncomfortable because there was no ceremony to guide him.

"Go on," Ike Myer said. "You're well known in the ward and you're well liked. I like you, and I think you can do the job. That's all that counts with me."

He and Ray signed the agreement, Ike's secretary witnessed it, his lawyer notarized it, and they all stood up, smiling. Ike offered the cigars to the lawyer, who declined, closing his briefcase, and to Ray, who took two. In addition to the money he put up, Ike Myer gave the building its new name.

Ray thought it was a middling joke; after all, it *was* a white elephant. However, to cut initial costs, no sign was ever erected, but the Yellow Pages of the city telephone directory did carry an italic listing under Taverns: *White Elephant, The.*

The White Elephant tavern opened for business on a Saturday in June of 1958 at three o'clock in the afternoon. A cardboard placard in the right front window, painted by Ray's unmarried sister Regina, who had taken some art courses, invited the general public to partake of free draft beer and a light lunch to celebrate the grand opening. It was an enormous success.

In the thirty years of his life, Ray Neery had only had two previous *great* days: in the summer of 1944, when he was sixteen and leader of the Steuben Park Gang, he whipped an eighteen-year-old tough in a fight that lasted half an hour, leaving the tough unable and unwilling to rise from the playground asphalt; Ray suffered two broken fingers and several loosened teeth. The other was the morning in January of 1952, when he was twenty-four. He continued to fire a water-cooled .30-caliber machine gun at attacking Chinese on the slope of a sub-zero, windswept ridge in Korea, despite the pain and shock of a grenade fragment lodged in his shinbone.

But those days were long past, no longer sufficiently real to him. Because of its intense immediacy, and because he enjoyed a distance of observation not possible in a fistfight or on a battlefield, the grand-opening celebration of his tavern was the richest moment of his existence.

The Greek's building was beautiful to look at.

To keep down Ike Myer's initial expenditure, Ray renovated the exterior himself. He borrowed ladders, a sandblaster, spray paint machinery, advice and occasional assistance from his many friends. He bound his head in a bandanna to keep his hair clean, covered his nose and mouth with a mask needed to keep his lungs free of infection, and climbed the rungs to strip off the dirty skin grown over the painted surface in the course of nearly thirty years. When it was cleaned to its brick bone, he gave it two coats of fresh new weather-resistant white paint. Puzzling over squares, levels, and miter cuts with a handsaw, he built three firm new wooden steps from the sidewalk to the front door.

He went home in the evenings to his parents' house so tired, his feet cramped with the shape of ladder rungs, hands clawed with the grip of a spray gun, his mind muddled with details, he had energy for no more than a bath, a cold bottle of beer, and supper before going to bed.

"You look like you're working for a living," his father, Timothy Neery, Sr., said to him one evening when his son came in. "You better come back to work for me. I'll pay you better and I'll leave a little life in you when you're through for the day."

"Never happen," Ray said. "There's a difference. I'm working for myself now, not just digging a hole for some Polack's garbage to float through."

"Francie telephoned, Ray," his mother said. But he was even too tired to call Frances Heenan, his girlfriend ever since his return from Korea. Frances went everywhere Ray went, so long as Ray let her.

She was in The White Elephant from the moment it opened for business that first day, and she was the one who locked the door at four-thirty Sunday morning when it closed on the very best of the three best days in Ray's life. She sat at the extreme far end of the bar, smoking mentholated cigarettes and watching Ray. She drank only three thin-stemmed glasses of blackberry brandy all night. She picked her own spot, and there were a few laughs about the barstool she used. She had painted its seat with phosphorescent gold paint, *Francie Heenan;* it glowed whenever she got up to visit the ladies room or replenish the supply of rye bread and raw beef with diced onions, the staple of the free lunch Ray gave to celebrate the opening.

She had a keen eye and took care of little things Ray forgot, like taking a razor blade and scraping off the little sticker marring the appearance of the huge new pane of Pittsburgh plate glass he delicately installed in the left front window. She also influenced his taste in the direction of moderation, persuading him that simple *Ladies* and *Gents* signs were preferable to *Kings* and *Queens* or *Setters* and *Pointers*.

When she wasn't busy with the free lunch, she watched Ray, and when he chose to speak to her, she listened. This was seldom, since the bar was packed with friends and family, and he worked deliberately, giving each customer a napkin *and* a coaster with the first drink.

Only when Ray's youngest brother—Billy Pat Neery, just turned twenty-one, recently separated from the Marine Corps and still living on mustering-out pay—volunteered to spell his brother behind the bar did Ray talk to her at length. He stopped drinking draft beer and shots of brandy, poured J & B Scotch over cracked ice, and took a Corina Lark from the small selection of cigars he stocked.

He felt resplendent. His hair was combed adroitly to decentralize his thinning crown, a hereditary Neery trait. He wore a white shirt, but with the collar unbuttoned, covering this with a black clip-on bow tie. For a professional touch he wore the red corduroy bartender's vest with silver buttons Francie Heenan presented him as a special gift. He lit the Corina expansively, rolling it between his fingers to ensure an even ash. Enthroning himself at the joint of back counter and bar, he leaned over to confide in his girlfriend.

"Will you look at that, Francie? Will you just look at them?"

"It's a terrific crowd, Ray," she said, anticipating what she thought he hoped to hear her say.

"Yeah. But how well off I am to be out of it. I could hug myself I'm so lucky. Half of them don't think one thought from one day into the next. God Almighty, I'm glad to be out of it!"

He meant all of them: the drifting, directionless ones, and the solid, stationary, stagnating ones who lacked his vision and sense of movement as well. He was only a tad kinder in his thoughts toward his family than to the others.

Ray came out from behind the bar, and while Francie watched him through the smoke from her cigarette, he circulated among his friends and customers, welcoming, shaking hands, accepting congratulations.

The bachelors, the ones who didn't know where they were going, gathered in and around the three stuffed red Naugahyde booths directly across from the bar, where the Greek's canned goods were once stacked. The booths were the work of Syzmanski, the upholsterer, called Irish, one of Ray's pals from Steuben Park days, who didn't know where he was going between upholstering jobs: furniture, convertible tops for automobiles, and the like. He had been explaining the difficulty of using nails with ornamental heads, but had finished, now resting himself against his cushions, steadily drinking bottled beer, arranging the empties in front of him in straight ranks.

"There's still free tap beer," Ray said. "What the hell are you paying for bottled for?"

"I got money," Syzmanski said. "Besides, I worked in the brewery once, you forget, for Pabst, they don't sterilize beer in barrels right."

They were holding two impromptu meetings at the same time. The Thibault brothers, Big and Little, were asking everyone to agree to form a fast-pitch softball team under the name of The White Elephant and enter it in the municipal athletic league that held games on Saturday mornings. "You ever seen me pitch fast-pitch?" said fat Big Thibault, the sometime new car salesman. He made room for himself, demonstrated the whip of his pitching arm. He enumerated the pitches he could handle: curve, drop, blooper, illegal sidearm concealed from an umpire's eyes.

"We'll walk off with the trophy," Little Thibault said. "The league's full of old men." He was still in his twenties, and lived off his older brother in the house they inherited jointly when their mother died. The Thibault boys prevailed, presented Ray with a demand that he sponsor the team, pay the league entry fee, and provide them with balls, bats, gloves, and uniform jerseys. Ray agreed, and Big Thibault said he'd get the necessary papers taken care of and bring them around to the tavern.

The other meeting was simultaneously and unsuccessfully conducted by Eddo Wandry, the Republican, who wanted recruits for a stock investment club he was forming. A charter was currently being drawn up.

Eddo had a college degree in business administration, had just taken a job with the General Electric branch plant in production scheduling. He objected to the black-on-yellow sticker Ray had on his cash register drawer that said *Help Stamp Out Republicans,* asking for equivalent space in Ray's front windows, where there were election posters for all the Democratic primary candidates.

Ray had to say hello twice to Jim Rickles, because Jim, a laid-off hydraulic press operator, was staring at Regina Neery's escort where they sat at the bar across the room. Jim loved Regina, and told her so whenever he had had enough to drink, but she never spoke to him because he was a hydraulic press operator and never read anything worthwhile.

"Who is that creep with her, Ray?" Jim Rickles asked.

"How should I know. Go tell Billy Pat to give you a drink on me. Be happy."

Ray had to squeeze his way through the crowd of strangers, friends of friends, to greet handsome Bob Magill the clotheshorse, who tried to live like he was Hugh Hefner. Handsome Bob was touching heads with a new girlfriend, both listening to "Ebbtide" on the big Seeburg jukebox as though it were Gypsy violins, holding hands, peeking at each other out of the corners of their eyes.

"This is Margie, Ray," handsome Bob said. The girls never said anything. Bob said, "This is Margie," or "This is Eileen," or "This is Toni," and he lit their cigarettes with flourish and bought them mixed drinks, looked with interest at the snapshots of old boyfriends and girlfriends and vacations they carried in their wallets. He made sixty dollars a week as assistant foreman in the laundry where all the old mothers and old maids and colored girls who ironed and packed laundry traded wisecracks and dirty jokes with him all day.

"Is she of age to be in here, Bob?" Ray whispered.

"Gimme a break, Ray," he said, leering with his eyebrows.

But Ray didn't have to worry about the law. Officer DaNunzio, the day beat cop, who'd known Ray and his family for twenty-five years, came over from the bar, carrying a water glass half-full of shelf-whiskey, to shake his hand. "It's a nice place, Ray. All this indirect lighting is like a nightclub. To think you run this place. I used to think when you was a kid you'd grow up to be a bum. Damned if I didn't! Bumps!" he said,

winked, toasted Ray with his glass, downed it, coughed, pushed back to
the bar for a taste of cold water to wash the burn out of his throat. Ray
knew he'd be in from time to time for his free glass of whiskey, loosen-
ing his pistol belt to get his breath in the summer heat. But no customers would get parking tickets near The White Elephant.

Ray went into the alcove, dodging the couples dancing there even
though Ray had a sign up saying he had no permit for dancing. He said
hello to Franklin Schrantz, who was tilting one of Ray's two pinball machines. Gambling on the machines, customer against the house, was
permissible. He especially wanted to talk to Franklin because he wanted
a professional opinion. Franklin Schrantz tended bar part-time for his
father.

"What do you think, Frank? A good draw for openers?"

"Fair. It's always good the first day if you give away beer and chow.
Wait and see." What the hell, Ray thought defensively, did Franklin
Schrantz know about it, working part-time for his father?

Franklin complained the pinball machine tilted too easily, and that
Ray had no bumper pool table installed. He claimed he could make a
fortune just playing bumper pool with strangers who didn't know his
skill, as people did in his father's tavern. Ray said he'd see about it.
Franklin, the smallest man in the bar at five feet two inches, took Ray's
arm and pulled him aside.

"Listen, Ray," he said. "There's some big son of a bitch there near the
door. Standing talking to your brother Tobin. There. I never saw him
before. I come walking to the bar for change from Billy Pat for the machine, he steps on my toe. On purpose. So help me, I'm walking past
him again, if he doesn't say he's sorry I'm gonna haul him out on the
street and hand him his head. I swear." Ray said to take it easy, he'd speak
to the man, straighten him out.

On his way to see the big man, who he thought he recognized, Dixon,
the permanently unemployed, came in. He explained to Ray he was
sorry for coming late, but he'd been downtown to a movie. He started to
tell Ray the plot. He hadn't worked since leaving the army in 1954, living
off his parents, seeing every movie that came to town. He began to de-
scribe the acting of Eva Marie Saint. Ray told him to get a drink on him.

The big man was talking to Ray's brother Tobin, and Tobin's wife,

Marion. He was saying that years ago everyone knew no one could whip Ray Neery in a fight, but he had fought him once anyhow, because in those days it was a matter of honor to fight when challenged; Ray called the man's father a sloppy drunk bastard, so he'd punched Ray straight in the nose and taken his beating.

"Tell that guy to go away, Ray," Marion said. "I can tell Toby's going to hit him." Ray said everything was all right, and bought all three a drink. But later, when the man left, Tobin, who often had fistfights, and went many Mondays to work inspecting sewer system construction for the city with swollen eyes, ears, and knuckles, followed him outside and knocked him down with his left hand, and Marion went around weeping and asking if her life was always going to be like that.

This was much later, after Ike Myer Jr. had come and gone, when many customers carried their bottles and glasses out on the sidewalk to escape the crush and heat and tobacco smoke, and to listen to Dixon, who imitated W. C. Fields and Chaplin and the sneering laugh of Doug Fairbanks Jr., having seen all three in many old movies on afternoon TV. There was a lot of drinking, and several persons simply threw their empty bottles and glasses into the gutter and street in front of the tavern.

Dixon only came inside long enough to get fresh drinks, and to request and receive permission from Ray to establish a bar tab, since he was short of cash at the present time.

Joe Neery, the youngest next to Billy Pat, had to leave early because his pregnant wife felt giddy, and because their babysitter might be having trouble with their two children, and because Joe had eaten six openfaced raw beef and onion sandwiches and now felt nauseated. He had a flat tire pulling away from the curb through all the jagged shards of bottles and glasses.

Ray's parents stood at the bar near the door. Timothy Sr. was very quiet until somebody finally asked him about the Depression, and he talked softly of his onetime membership in the IWW, and of the day he shook Bill Haywood's hand, ending by saying it was impossible, no matter what he said, to make young people today know what the Depression had really been like. "It's a shame Timmy can't see this," he said to Ray, referring to Timothy Neery Jr., killed in Korea the same week Ray was wounded. Then he was silent again.

"Sure, sure," Ray said, not liking the inappropriate mention of death. He put his arm around his mother, formidable in her corset, her hair rinsed a crackling metallic blue. She made him smell her corsage. She wore her Gold Star Mother's pin next to it.

Ray's unmarried sister Regina complained because she couldn't order a champagne cocktail. Ordinarily she went downtown when she had a drink. Her escort this night was an oboist in the city symphony. They discussed mobiles.

"Ray," she said, tightening the cords in her throat, uncrossing her nyloned knees, "will you *please* go tell that damn Rickles to stop gaping at me!"

"I'll go talk to him if you want me to," her escort, younger, blond, and yet more balding than Ray, said.

"Ignore him," Regina said. Ray bought them a round.

He had a technical conversation with Rollie Hackbarth, his sister Annie's husband. Rollie owned and operated *Rollie's,* a prosperous bar in the Puerto Rican district. Rollie had been listening carefully to Eddo Wandry's ideas on a stock investment club. He admired the tile floor Ray laid himself—easy to clean—and questioned him on the arrangements he had with liquor suppliers, vending jobbers, and his boss Ike Myer Jr.

"He's not my boss. We have a loose written agreement. I'm the management," Ray said.

"How'll you heat it in winter?"

"I plan on putting in an oil burner in the back alcove."

"You've got to admit it's nice," Annie said to her husband, and Rollie said *Umm* with his lips closed tight.

Ray tried to go back to work behind the bar, but he was so unsteady from brandies and scotches he bumped his knee painfully against the wash tank and dropped and broke the fifth of blackberry brandy he tried to pick up, so he promised Billy Pat a sawbuck if he'd tend bar the rest of the night. Billy Pat poured himself another scotch over ice after Ray rejoined Frances Heenan.

"Look at them, Francie," he said. "What in the hell becomes of them? Dixon. Irish. Rickles. What do they ever do with themselves?"

"I guess they settle down and get married and have kids, like your brothers," she said, watching him.

"Goddamnit," he said, "the responsibility I've got now with this place, I can't tie one hand behind my back getting married now."

"I know," she said, and blew smoke toward the ceiling.

"Am I glad to be the hell out of that!" he said, looking at his opening night crowd.

The high point of the evening was the arrival of Ike Myer Jr., who came wearing khaki slacks, sandals, and an aloha shirt. He was known to everyone since his picture was often in the newspaper as elections drew nearer. He reached across the bar to shake hands with Ray, bought a round of drinks for the house, smiled a great deal, and lit but did not smoke the cigar Ray offered him.

"I'm a little tight," Ray said to him.

"Well why not? This is your inauguration here. I guess tight, and why the hell not?" He left soon afterward in his mint 1941 Lincoln Continental, a millionaire's affectation he planned on getting rid of before the year was out. Very few people knew how badly he wanted to be governor in 1960.

Billy Pat and Francie Heenan shooed people out when legal closing time came at three-thirty in the morning. The married people with children left much earlier. Irish Syzmanski the upholsterer had to be carried out by the Thibault brothers. Dixon urged Ray not to miss the Eva Marie Saint movie. Handsome Bob Magill left holding hands with Margie, winking to Billy Pat behind her back. Jim Rickles left to follow Regina Neery and her oboist. On his last play of the pinball machine, Franklin Schrantz won thirty dollars from the house. A taxicab had to be called for Officer DaNunzio, who insisted as he was helped out by the cabbie that all those kids at Steuben Park had been a bunch of god-damned little bums for as long as he'd known them. Eddo Wandry asked Ray to keep the stock investment club in mind.

Ray was too drunk to count his receipts or do any cleaning up that night. He went out the door leaning on Billy Pat's arm while Francie Heenan turned the key in the lock. "Just name one person here tonight who's got one damn thing in the world—or a chance of it! Name one," he said to his brother.

"Your mom and dad," Francie said from behind him.

"What are you talking about?" Ray said. "Their life is over already for Christ's sakes!"

The original plan was to open every day at eleven-thirty in the morning. It was just past three in the afternoon when Ray woke up the next day, unable to remember if he'd set his alarm clock when he crawled into bed or not. He tried to spring up, was hit between and behind the eyes by his dry, stony hangover, so lay back and called for his youngest brother.

"If it ain't ghost who walks," Billy Pat said from the doorway.

"Cut it out. Do me a favor, will you? Find my keys. They must be in my pants or on the dresser someplace. Go down and open up for me." He imagined a throng milling angrily before the locked door. "I feel like holy hell. Give me this one break, will you? My head's killing me. I'll be down before long."

He allowed himself the luxury of another hour's half-sleep before rising slowly to swallow aspirins and grab a hot shower.

His mother set out orange juice, bacon and eggs, and coffee on the kitchen table for him. He listened to the church bells ringing for the ladies' sodality, and had just begun to eat, still dehydrated but alive, when Billy Pat came into the house.

"What are you doing here? Who's at the tavern?"

"Nobody," Billy Pat said, "that's why I came back. Christ, Ray, it's Sunday. It's like a tomb in there. It was really getting to me. Why don't you get a used TV in there? Anyway, I swept it up a little for you."

So the hours were changed. Ray opened The White Elephant every day at three-thirty in the afternoon. And still that was too early. One afternoon he sat behind the bar, the place spotless, listening to the Seeburg and drinking scotch from three-thirty till nine that evening when Packy Mitchell, a retired prizefighter on the skids, came in, sheepish and humble, to ask him for credit.

And he granted it, just to have someone to talk to. Francie was helping with inventory nights in the office where she worked that week, or else at least she'd have been there. One Tuesday afternoon he determined not to put money in the jukebox just to test his will power, and the only sound all afternoon was the telephone. Eddo Wandry called to give him one last chance to join his investment club.

Ray said no. Ike Myer was sending out dollars in search of their brothers. He was glad to see Officer DaNunzio whenever he came in to use the toilet and drink a free whiskey. The first time his liquor jobber checked in on him, all he ordered was some scotch.

"Greetings and salutations!" Dixon said when he came in one afternoon at four o'clock. He had just come from a matinee rerun of an early Disney movie downtown.

"Hello, Dix," was all Ray said. With the blinds down over the windows, it was very dark inside The White Elephant, the Seeburg and the pinball lights glowing. Ray sat behind the bar with his chin on his hands. Water dripped from the tap into the empty wash tank, and there was a full ashtray before Ray on the bartop.

"Come on, Ray, I'm not the world's greatest, but I got feelings. Crack a smile why don't you?"

"I was thinking," Ray said, "how much it would set me back to get a used television set."

He bought a used Muntz and put it on a shelf in the corner, where it could be seen from any place at the bar or either of the three booths. Dixon came in every day at three-thirty when Ray opened up. They drank together, and watched the TV. There was a soap opera from three-thirty to four, an early movie at four about which Dixon made critical commentary, and after the movie Douglas Edwards came on to talk about the condition of the nation and the world. It was comforting to sit back, lazy and radiant with their drinks, and listen to Doug Edwards speak.

"I swear I don't feel at ease until he tells me so every day," Dixon said.

"You ready?" Ray said, reaching for Dixon's brand, Charter Oak.

"Might's well. I'm not going downtown tonight. All the features are changing tomorrow though. Put that on my tab, will you, Ray? I insist we have this one on my tab."

After she fixed dinner for herself and her father, Francie Heenan came to sit on her personalized stool, nurse a glass of blackberry brandy, and watch Ray.

The Thibault boys made good their threat. They organized a fast-pitch softball team. Ray managed and footed the bill. Games were every Saturday morning at a city athletic field across town. Big Thibault called for him in his Ford demonstrator early in the morning. They loaded the trunk with two canvas bags of equipment, dressed in the green and white White Elephant colors, picked up Francie at her father's house on the way to the game. It was a tavern league, the losers of each game obliged to buy the beer for the winners at the losers' sponsoring bar. Over the season, The White Elephant won five and lost five. Sometimes Big Thibault's control on the mound was excellent, sometimes not.

The parties after the games were long and drunken, so on his winning days Ray didn't get to open his tavern until late in the evening, after several couples and groups of friends had driven slowly past the darkened building, peering at the windows for a light. A few even stopped and tried the locked door. Losing a game was just that much out of Ray's pocket, in addition to a rowdy atmosphere that kept a lot of neighborhood people away.

One Saturday, handsome Bob Magill walked through the door with a new girl in tow. He was dressed to kill, his breath sweet with clove Lifesavers. The scent of his girl's perfume throbbed in the late August evening air. The highlights in her lacquered hair danced.

"Jesus," handsome Bob said to her. "I mean, it's actually really a nice place. The guy runs it's a friend of mine." He tried to wake Ray up.

The celebration had left its mark. Ray was sleeping head down on his hands on the bartop. His hair was ruffled and spiked, his creeping baldness showing. Around him, like stars in a halo, were overflowing ashtrays. The entire bartop was littered with crushed cigarette packages, spilled drink puddles, glasses, and beer bottles. The stink of tobacco smoke seemed to seep out of the walls and fixtures. Ray wasn't the only one sleeping.

There were two sleepers in each of the three booths. Big and Little Thibault occupied the one nearest the door. On the table between them was a large, cold, and half-consumed pizza pie. In the second, Irish Syzmanski rested his head on the cushions he had himself upholstered. Across from him, Dixon snored. In the third booth, Jim Rickles, the good-field-no-hit second baseman, fluttered his eyelashes. His partner's face was turned away, but handsome Bob thought it was Billy Pat Neery. In the alcove, his back against the two dusty bags of softball gear, lay Franklin Schrantz, clutching a twenty-dollar bill he'd won on the pinball machine to his left before passing out.

"It's usually real nice, actually," handsome Bob said to his date.

"Let's go, OK?" she said. Three people were staring at her, members of the winning team. They sat on stools, sullen and bleary-eyed next to Francie Heenan's personalized stool, grotesque in purple and white, sweated and dried softball jerseys, *Emil's Tap* on their chests. One dug another in the ribs and nodded toward Bob's girl. The third wiped his mouth on the short sleeve of his jersey, focused his eyes on her.

"Ray," handsome Bob said, shaking him gingerly, "how's about a little service." Ray lifted his head, one-eyed. "This is Fay," Bob said. Fay said nothing, looked away from the three rude ballplayers. "What do you want to drink, Fay?" he asked his girl.

"Whiskey sour," she murmured.

"Two whiskey sours, Ray," handsome Bob said.

"Will you get the goddamn hell out of here!" Ray said. "Can't you see I'm sick!" He lowered his head. They left just as Francie Heenan came out of the ladies' room. She meant to call them back, but one of Emil's ballplayers reached for her waist, and she had to dodge.

"Hurrah!" the ballplayer shouted, groping. "She's back!"

"Come here and let me buy you a drink, sweets," another said.

"Ray, wake up," Francie said. "Go in and wash your face and get this place cleaned up."

"Did you hear that, Francie?" Ray said as he got up and came out from behind the bar. "Magill asks me for a whiskey sour. What is this, uptown? Fay!" he snorted. Handsome Bob never brought his girls to The White Elephant again.

"Hey, boss," one of Emil's men said, "tell that woman not to be so un-social."

"How would you like me to punch you out," Ray said. The three Emil's players sized Ray up, sized up the sleeping men in the booths. Jim Rickles and Dixon were showing signs of life. Emil's players left and of course also never returned.

"Wash your face, Ray," Francie said.

At the end of August, Francie took an afternoon off work, went to see a doctor, and learned she was two months pregnant. She and Ray drove across the state line one night after he closed up, and were married by a

justice of the peace. Under the circumstances, there was no formal celebration, but Ike Myer Jr. gave them a cut-glass punchbowl set, ladle and
a dozen cups, for a wedding present. Some jokes were made: *now* he'd
really settle down; regular meals and he'd be as fat as Big Thibault or his
brother Joe; he had someone to see he got to work on time now!

His mother said to her husband that with only Billy Pat and Regina
living at home the house felt empty.

Then people started going places. Dixon met a girl, a waitress, married her after only two weeks, and moved out of the neighborhood.
Eddo Wandry got promoted to bonus row at General Electric, was seen
only on Sunday afternoons at Rollie's, where his stock investment club
met; they were showing twelve and a half percent on their money, had
made a pile on American Motors. Franklin Schrantz argued over salary
with his father, so went to Kansas City, where he enrolled in an airline
ticket agent training course.

DaNunzio retired, and the new cop on the beat ticketed Ray's customers for overparking, warned him about serving underage college
students, and pinched him twice for permitting gambling on the prem-
ises. Ike Myer paid the fines and told him to get rid of the pinball machines.

Big Thibault, only thirty-six years old, died quickly one night of a
seizure after drinking and eating to excess, and it was rumored his
younger brother, brooding after the funeral, no longer left their inherited house, lived in a growing heap of his own garbage.

And Regina Neery, who never came to The White Elephant because
people like her brother Tobin picked fights there, and faced with spin-
sterhood, married Jim Rickles, the hydraulic press operator. Ike Myer Jr.
gave them a modern painting for their apartment living room. Tobin
Neery, to stop his wife's nagging, went on the water wagon.

In the statewide elections of November 1958, the Democrats made
great inroads, winning every state office except those of governor and
lieutenant governor.

In January of the new year, Francie told Ray to ask Ike Myer for more
money.

"Are you joking, Francie? I owe that man my life. Where would I be without him? He keeps on shelling out and shelling out, he's liable to throw me out on my ear. You can only try a man's patience so far. I owe him too much already."

"You owe me something too. You'd better ask him, or I will," she said. She still watched him carefully as she had before their marriage, still spent every evening on her special stool in The White Elephant, but she no longer waited until he felt like speaking to speak to him. When she thought he was drinking too much, she told him so, even if he didn't stop.

Ray asked his sponsor for more money, and was, unemotionally, refused.

"How am I supposed to live? The baby's going to cost. What do you expect of me, Ike?"

"A profit. It's that simple. We'd work out some ideas for the place if I wasn't so busy with the party. I don't have to tell you things are popping right now. It's a shame you didn't have time to stay with the committee. The guy took your spot is strictly no good, but he has friends upstate."

"No more money then, is that right?" Ray said. He had lost interest in politics.

"That's what the man said. Come on now, don't disappoint me. Here, take a handful of these cigars with you, Ray. I never smoke the things."

For a while, he tried pleasing them both, but one night made up his mind for him. Dixon stopped in with his wife, who was also pregnant, and the four of them had several drinks at the bar. Dixon laid a twenty on the bar to cover the rounds. While his wife was in the ladies' and Dixon was putting change into the cigarette machine next to the Seeburg, Francie whispered to her husband.

"Ask him for what he owes you."

"For what?" Ray said. He was on his sixth scotch of the evening.

"His bar bill. He's working. He's got money. Tell him to pay you."

"Not now, Frances."

"Why not?"

"Just not now. Christ, I haven't seen him for a couple months. You don't just bug him to pay his tab. He's my friend."

"I said ask now," Francie said. She clawed in her purse for her cigarette lighter.

"No."

"No?" She dropped the lighter back into her purse.

"No. Not if hell freezes over." Ray swallowed his drink.

"If hell freezes over what?" Dixon asked, returning to the bar.

"Please call me a cab, Raymond," Francie said. She put away her cigarettes, pushed the half-finished blackberry brandy away from her, got carefully off her stool.

"Hey, where you going?" Dixon said.

"For the Christ's sakes, Francie—"

"Please call me a cab."

She continued to live with him only until the night of the fire, two weeks after she returned from the hospital with their newborn daughter.

To save fuel, Ray turned the oil heater off when he closed at night, then lit it the next afternoon when he came in at three-thirty. Once it was going, he hopped around it, warming his hands, shuddering with the cold air that set into the building overnight. A cold mass of Canadian air had swept over the city after a frontal snow storm, remained there. Many people remembered the month as one in which cars would not start.

It was a cheap but powerful heater. Ray knew what he was doing the night in late February he left it on. It was a quarter past three, and he had just pushed Packy Mitchell the old fighter out the front door. He turned it up as high as it would go, then left, locking up with a narrow smile on his face. It overheated, exploded. The fire was through the roof before the engine companies responded.

There was some concern for the first twenty minutes that it might spread to the outbuildings of the padlock and chain factory in the rear, but the firemen brought it under control. Fortunately for Ike Myer Jr., the building was more than adequately insured.

"I'm disappointed in you, Ray," he said when they dissolved their agreement. Ike Myer Jr. suspected, and Francie knew, so she moved back to her father's house with their infant daughter, filing for divorce.

"No regrets here, Francie," Ray said. "I'm sorry."

"All I regret is seven years out of my life."

Timothy Neery Sr. got his son back into the union by paying a fifty-dollar bribe to the official Ray nearly defeated for office once. He went back to manning the decompression chamber on tunnel construction. He drank a lot and put on a good deal of weight.

His father didn't like the divorce, said he was glad Timothy Jr. wasn't there to see that, but his mother was glad to have him back in the house again. Regina Rickles had broken off all contact with her family, though they knew she was expecting a baby.

Billy Pat told a friend, "My oldest bro's a jerk. All he does is sit and watch daytime television when he's not working or sitting in a tavern." Tobin tried unsuccessfully to get him to go on the wagon, but Ray didn't listen to people.

He called in sick to work one day and went on a minor bender that nearly cost him his job and union ticket. "You know," he said to Nicky Anagnos, the proprietor of *Little Nick's Streamlined Bar,* "the trouble is I just want to just be a bum." But sometimes he remembered the day in Korea when he was a hero, and once he argued politics, picked a fight, and got his clock cleaned in the alley behind Nick's by a much younger man.

As for Ike Myer Jr., he compromised with the upstate delegations and was nominated for lieutenant governor of the state in 1960. He turned the Greek's building into a tangible asset on his books, too. In 1961, after it had sat, a white shell, its innards charred, broken, burned-through roof beams exposed like black ribs, the city took it off his hands at a very good price. Urban renewal was in full swing. Ike's ticket lost the election by a whisker—upstate swung Republican—so he abandoned politics to concentrate on lucrative municipal-funded development projects.

Today, where The White Elephant once stood is an expanse of concrete and grass, an expressway cloverleaf interchange. Motorists drive past the former site at fifty-five miles an hour.

Dirt

"Dirt," my mother often said while cleaning house, "you fight it all your life, and when you're dead they throw it in your face."

The scalloped edge of the pale blue canopy snapped in the wind, very close to Father Daley's high, natural pompadour. The long unpressed skirt of his black gown whipped around his legs until he held it still with the same hand that held the little book. He half-knelt at the end of the open grave and picked up some of the moist, light-brown clay in his fingers. We all waited, our weeping slacked, for him to stand again, and I wondered if his head would touch the canopy as he rose. He didn't touch the canopy; he took a long step backwards, like a child playing Captain-May-I?, as if he meant to wind up and throw the clay a great distance over our heads, across the flat green cemetery lawn.

He let go his skirt to look again in the book, perhaps not trusting to memory for the words. His other arm made short, rhythmic practice swings as he read. The warm May wind blew his gown and snapped the edge of the canopy, and we listened to what he said. "Dust thou art, and unto dust thou return," he read. He tossed the clay, underhand, in three even motions as he finished reading the passage.

It scattered, some of it dropping back onto the heaped parapet of earth where he'd picked it up, some rolling into the short space between the casket and the parapet, dropping all the way into the bottom of the grave, some of it falling among the flowers, two large mounted sprays labeled *Mother* and *Grandmother* with wide white bands of glossy ribbon. Some dropped onto the lid of my mother's casket. We resumed our weeping.

Father Daley had more to say. The book looked too small to be a Bible, perhaps a condensed volume, something handy for baptisms and marriages and funerals, burials. He read on. He was too tall and young and handsome to be very effective. His ceremony seemed self-consciously uncertain, for my mother had no formal religion. But my brother Len and his wife sent their daughter to St. Mark's Episcopal, and we wanted someone, so the assistant pastor was pressed into duty. But Father Daley had a nice voice. He looked like a man with an ecclesiastical future, and he read more words.

He spoke about man born of woman being of few days, and those full of trouble. Man was like a flower in bloom, soon cut down. A shadow that fled and did not continue. Words.

But I had seen the dirt. Up until that moment I knew exactly what to do, think, feel, but not anymore. I think I was the first to stop crying.

There was a very hot, very clear sky, an expanse of fresh green dotted with flush grave markers of pebbled bronze that did not reflect the sun, and here under a canopy, a grave, casket, flowers, Father Daley reading, my sister, three brothers, wives, children, relatives, friends, my wife and myself. The words stopped and there was just the wind, people moving out under the sun again to leave, and I was grateful for my wife's arm through mine to guide me. She gave me a clean handkerchief and I blew my nose and wondered what to do, think, feel next.

It had been a long ride from the funeral home to the cemetery. A helmeted motorcycle policeman led the black Cadillac hearse to be sure traffic stopped at intersections to let the whole of our procession pass safely through. I drove my father-in-law's Ford because he rode in a car directly behind the hearse with the other pallbearers. My wife and her mother were with me, but we didn't speak except that my mother-in-law said what a beautiful day it was. We didn't answer her, her voice still soft with the solemnity of the brief service Father Daley conducted at the funeral home.

The Episcopalians, my brother Len told me, don't usually include personal eulogies at funerals, but Father Daley was kind enough to depart from doctrine and speak of my mother by name, to mention her family; he referred to notes as he spoke in the parlor before her open casket, but even then he made several mistakes, once referring to my sister Jane as if she were my aunt, my mother's sister.

After the eulogy was over and the funeral director ushered us into an antechamber while his assistants removed my mother's glasses and jewelry and closed the casket, my brother came and asked me if I thought it was all right, had it been too Episcopalian in any way. I assured him, my wife assured him, my sister and my other two brothers assured him, it had been fine, just what we had wanted.

At the huge stone and ironwork cemetery entrance the policeman left us. Easter was not long past, so there were flowers on nearly all the graves, their colors washed dull by weather, ribbons limp. Little American flags on sticks marked the veterans here and there in the wide stretches of bright green grass. The cemetery was not old, so had no stone monuments or mausoleums except in one remote section where my sister told me plots were very expensive. We drove the long winding way slowly over the narrow graveled road. Sometimes I looked in the rearview mirror and saw the headlights of the car behind me glowing superfluously in the blazing day. We reached our section and I pulled the car to the right side of the road and parked.

I got out and opened the doors for my wife and mother-in-law, closed them carefully behind them, not wanting to make an unseemly noise. We stood, all of us, next to the line of cars, and waited for the pallbearers to lead the way to the grave site. I looked down toward the hearse and recognized my father-in-law's back. The grave was a good way in from the road, almost at the fence surrounding the cemetery. The fence was hidden by double, at times triple, rows of evergreens. The blue three-sided canopy looked like a bazaar tent set on a public green for a holiday.

The pallbearers took the casket from the hearse and started toward it.

They carried it awkwardly, their free hands extended from their bodies like a troupe of tightrope walkers straining for balance. The funeral director assisted them at one end. He was a very efficient man.

He was tall, and must have used a sunlamp for his even tan, had distinguished, rich iron-gray hair at his temples. The previous night and that morning he had been with us always, there at my shoulder if I turned with a question, to lean forward discreetly and whisper just the right answer. Ahead of him now, his two assistants carried the two largest floral tributes to put on the casket once it was over the open grave. They were identical young men, blond, with crew-cuts and prominent chins. In the funeral parlor they stood in corners with their feet set apart, hands clasped behind their backs; when the director sent them on errands or they carried in flowers, they moved as quickly and quietly as cats. They had faces that didn't change expression, eyes that never blinked.

The women held their hats on their heads because of the wind, and my mother-in-law moved away from us, following the pallbearers. My wife took my arm. "Come on now," she said, "you have to be up front. Do you want a handkerchief?"

"No," I said. I didn't think I would cry anymore. There had been weeping the night before when my family went to the parlor to view my mother's body for the first time, when we stood in front of the casket and wept and said how beautiful and peaceful and *real* she looked, until we had to stop and move away and admire all the flowers that had been sent. And the rest of the night we were busy, meeting those who came to see her, telling them how much we appreciated their coming, agreeing, yes, it was a very sudden, unexpected thing, taking them up to the casket, nodding, yes, she did look so peaceful, but by then not thinking it looked like her anymore. Friends of mine had to be introduced to my sister and brothers, to each other, questions had to be answered. We stayed until eleven o'clock just in case someone should come late.

The visitors wrote their names in the director's guest book, and we took this home with us, exhausted, to look over as we had a last cup of coffee before sleeping. I remember we talked about one man who went so far as to cross himself and say a prayer at my mother's casket, and someone mentioned another man who had tears in his eyes who declined to go look at the body because he wanted to remember her the way she was in life. And still another, a lady who hadn't seen my mother in fifteen years, but had her son drive her sixty miles to pay her respects. Such things made us feel better.

As I was falling asleep that night, I thought to myself what a good thing funerals are, the help they give us; I caught myself trying to remember all the names in the visitors' book, because my mother would surely like to know who came, as if she wasn't really dead after all.

My wife made me walk quickly to the front of the people following the pallbearers so I would be under the canopy with my sister and brothers. I looked at them as I passed, friends and relatives, until I understood they didn't want to look at me, and then I kept my eyes on the ground and saw we were following traces left by the wheels of the grave-digging machine in the grass where it had gone to and from the road to the grave site. When we were under the canopy someone began to cry just behind me, even before Father Daley had taken his place at the head of the casket. And so we all wept again.

We wept that morning at the service in the funeral home, sitting in even rows of straight-backed chairs, like students at a lecture, surrounded by flowers in pots wrapped in gold paper, flowers along the walls on metal stands, flowers banked on both sides of my mother's casket, hearing young Father Daley say that life was only three-score and ten years, and even if a man was strong and lived four-score years, still it came to this end. My wife had put handkerchiefs in my jacket pockets because she knew I would weep, and I used one and then the other, listening to the Episcopalian priest and looking at the back of my father-in-law's neck where he sat in front of me in the first row with the pallbearers.

Now we all wept again under the canopy, for the last time, I thought, because this was the last ritual. My oldest brother, Nils, who is over forty, cried like a small boy, my brothers Milt and Len, my sister Jane, my wife sniffling and clutching the crook of my elbow tightly, offering me her handkerchief. Father Daley took his place at the head of the casket, looked at all our faces for silence, and we controlled ourselves, wept less openly, and he began to speak again, another short eulogy, several prayers I heard as dimly as I saw through my smeared eyes.

I gave the handkerchief back to my wife and folded my hands in front of me and made myself wait, only wait for it to end. I closed my eyes to stop the tears, sensing the casket, the odor of flowers, close to us, the heat and wind and sky, the people, children, Father Daley's voice. Then came the words . . . the dirt.

My wife led me back to the car. "We shouldn't have rolled the windows up," she said, "it's roasting in there by now." It ended very quickly.

The distinguished and efficient funeral director spoke to my sister, then disappeared into the empty hearse. His assistants began to strike the canopy and fold up the artificial grass mats that concealed the fresh earth around the grave. Father Daley closed his little book and God blessed my three brothers and their wives. Women held their hats on their heads. Men stepped away from the grave site and lit cigarettes, looked for clouds in the burning sky. Children, my nieces and nephews, held their parents' hands and began to ask how soon they could leave.

"At least it's over," I said. "I want to get home."

"We have to go to Jane's, honey," my wife said. It was not over. There would be a light lunch at Jane's, drinks. I saw my sister shaking Father Daley's hand, no doubt inviting him. There would be paper napkins and paper plates balanced on knees when the TV tables gave out, and talk, conversation, reminiscing. People moved to their cars, said goodbye; it was nice to have seen each other again even though it was for such a sad occasion. I looked back at the grave site.

A man wearing overalls came out from the trees near the fence where he must have been waiting. He carried two shovels. My wife's parents approached us. The man stuck the shovels into the pile of dirt exposed now that the canopy and the mats were gone. The assistants took the flowers off the casket and joined the director at the hearse. The overalled man was joined by another dressed like himself. They put their hands on their hips and looked at the casket, waiting to start. I didn't look anymore for fear they might spit on their hands before taking up the shovels.

"Do you want a clean hankie?" my wife asked me.

"No," I said, but I was weeping again, and took it.

"I've got another one if you need it," she said.

"The damn dirt," I said as I got into the back seat of my father-in-law's car, seat covers scorching hot. My in-laws were careful not to appear to be listening to me, not noticing me at all.

"What?" my wife said, but I didn't repeat it. The trouble is, I thought, the trouble is it's the dirt. The damn dirt. All the rest is talk, words. That's the end of it. The damn dirt. As my mother used to say.

Psychic Friends

I had not thought death had undone so many.

—T. S. Eliot

Zilligen passed the house at least a dozen times on the long feckless walks he took to break the tedium of his empty days—he could only stand so much television before gagging on talk shows and soap operas, sit only so long over coffee in fast-food outlets, pretend to read newspapers and periodicals no more than an hour or two in the company of winos and addicts taking shelter at the public library. So he knew the house, one of his personal landmarks in the aged, weary neighborhood he moved into to play out such days or years as were left to him. But he had not truly *looked* at it before.

It was a house like any other on the block, two stories that seemed to sag and lean a couple of degrees, a large porch, windows opaque with dull curtains, the whole of it crying out for repainting, rejuvenation. Cracked, uneven flagstones led Zilligen from the sidewalk to worn porch steps, where he paused. Two plots of weedy grass needed mowing. A flower bed gaped, void of plants. Some variety of stunted, untrimmed shrubbery partially masked the gray foundation stones. It was the sign that stopped him on this day's walk. Why had he not noted it before?

It was a large sign, resting on two struts meant to anchor it, he supposed, in the yard, but it was propped against the porch railing, slightly tilted. *Reader,* it said in very large letters at the top. At the bottom, smaller letters: *Madam Auchmunty.* In the middle, dominating, was a huge stylized hand, garish orange to approximate flesh tone, raised palm outward like a traffic signal commanding halt. The lines in the palm were drawn in black, like rivers on a map.

He ought, Zilligen thought, to have his head examined, but doubted his bare-bones health insurance covered that.

Then he mounted the steps, felt them give a little under his shoes, creak, then crossed the porch to the door, boards echoing, found the doorbell, pressed it. He heard no ring or buzz, no sound of movement inside, was ready to turn away, leave, when he caught the flutter of curtain behind the nearest streaked window, and the door opened with a lurch. The woman's face seemed to show irritation, impatience—he had disturbed, was intruding.

She said, "Yes." It was more statement than question.

Zilligen said, "You're the reader? On the sign? Madam Auchmunty?"

"Yes," she said, and stood back, swung the door fully open, and Zilligen entered, though she uttered no word of invitation, as if, he thought, he was expected, had a long-standing appointment. He followed her into the living room.

It was an absolutely ordinary house, a little dim with such light as penetrated the nondescript curtains, a little cluttered with bric-a-brac on shelves and end tables, books here and there, doilies on the arms of the couch and overstuffed chairs, maybe a little dirty, but that was only a feeling Zilligen got. It smelled strongly of something indistinct cooking in a distant kitchen, an odor only minimally nauseating. He expected two chairs, a table they would face each other across, but she gestured him to a seat on the sofa that made a whooshing sound, gave a few inches beneath him when he sat.

"Yes," she said again, as if he had correctly obeyed complicated instructions.

Madam Auchmunty was an ordinary-looking woman, at least Zilligen's age. Her gray-streaked hair pulled back and clipped at her nape, she wore a loose housecoat, the sort of thing Zilligen's mother dressed in to clean or cook fifty years ago. She was overweight, just enough to make her formidable. Her eyes, magnified by spectacles, were blank. The crepey skin of her neck dotted with tiny moles, a dusting of mustache on her upper lip, faint fuzz on her chin—somebody's unpleasant granny, Zilligen thought, glad he was not close enough to smell her. He considered standing, striding out the door.

She said, "Yes," once more, and then, before he could formulate any response, "You have questions?"

Zilligen tried to smile, look casual, said, "I'm not really so sure about this . . ." He lifted a hand to the room, toward her, slapped his knee lightly to include himself.

She said, "Natural enough." And she said, "Listen to me here a minute," and, "You're more confused than doubting at this instant. You half-expected me to wear a turban on my head, maybe a crystal ball? Do I look like a Gypsy?" Zilligen shook his head. "You half-expected mood music coming out of the walls, incense, candles, all the triteness, and when you don't find that you don't know what to think, do you?" He didn't like her voice: strict, bossy, like the old-maid teachers Zilligen suffered as a boy.

"That's pretty close," he said, and, "See, I'm here on a sort of whim. I saw your sign. Call me curious," he said.

Madam Auchmunty smiled, a grin showing stained teeth, let a harumph out, said, "Let me clarify for you if I may." Zilligen sat back into the sofa's cushions. Madam Auchmunty straightened up on her chair, squared her shoulders, lifted her fuzzy chin, breathed deep, exhaled a sigh, then spoke as if reading a prepared lecture.

She said, "As to doubts concerning my authenticity, allow me to tell you something of yourself based only on certain obvious . . . *vibrations* is an adequate word."

"My aura," Zilligen said. "I know some of the jargon."

"Please don't interrupt," she said, and, "You are of course skeptical of me because you are by temperament, by nature, a skeptic. I suspect you have transformed yourself over your adult years into a full-fledged cynic? Yet you are interested to know things. I see you have entered an advanced, perhaps the final, phase of your life. You clearly carry great burdens in the form of despair at what has transpired in your existence, and you wish for . . . you *hope* for relief."

"That sort of stuff," Zilligen said, near anger, "you could say about just about everybody." He decided he didn't like her, actively disliked her, tensed his legs to stand, leave. He didn't have money to throw away on this!

"Religion," she said, "is the solution for some, but you're not religious. Never were. Therapy of whatever variety can work wonders, but not for you, you consider that all guff. You don't believe in reincarnation. You don't believe in clairvoyance. You don't believe in the afterlife. You scoff at astrology and tea leaves. And there isn't a soul on earth you can confide in, is there?"

Zilligen drooped, could not have stood if he wanted to. He shivered, swallowed. He said, "That's pretty good. Is that what you do with . . . you call them *clients*, I suppose? Just look at them and start in popping out with things?"

Madam Auchmunty said, "I work in any number of modes, depending. I do *not* read palms, the sign's just an announcement the laity can understand easily. I do *not* foretell the future, so don't ask me to recommend horses to bet on or stocks to buy. I cannot tell you when you will die, if that's what's eating you. And I hasten to say I do *not* accept any and all . . . *clients* who come to my door."

"Will you accept me?" Zilligen heard himself say. It felt like a long silence before she answered him.

"I must ponder it," she said. And, "Go. Give me at least a few days. Return and I'll know *if* I wish to work with you, and *how, if,* that is, I decide in your favor." She stood.

Zilligen stood, said, "Why would you possibly not want to take me on?"

"You're not a very nice man, are you," she said, and led him to the door, opened it, stood aside.

"My name's Zilligen, August J.," he said.

"I knew your name, Mr. Zilligen," she said, "when you came to my door." And then he was outside, down her creaky porch steps, on the sidewalk, trembling a little, feeling laughter tickle the back of his palate, uncertain if he was thrilled or just ashamed of himself.

He waited two days before returning, maybe the hardest days in all the months since the string of disasters that brought him to this dead end he wasn't sure he could hack. Lacking patience with television and the library's reading room, he walked more often and farther than ever before. To occupy his mind, Zilligen took to counting his calamities, ticking them off, over and over, on the fingers of his memory, a kind of chanting that, repeated enough, he hoped, rendered them neutral, so much babble.

On his sixty-third birthday, as if there were malevolent magic in the number, his long-time employer, a high-risk auto, casualty, and life insurance provider, was taken over without warning by an out-of-state conglomerate. Zilligen, a claims specialist, was downsized out the door without ceremony, his pension significantly devalued.

He figured to cope, grabbed his Social Security, counted on his V.A. benefits in the event of long-term or catastrophic illness, but then his wife of forty years hit him with her whammy. Claiming she'd contemplated the action from the moment their only child, then age nineteen, left home twenty years ago, she gave him the boot with a vengeance. She won her suit on grounds of extreme mental cruelty and neglect, putting forth preposterous lies that convinced a gullible family court judge, who told Zilligen from the bench he deserved to spend his remaining days contemplating the flaws in his character and personality, and the harm and hurt he had done those closest to him.

The judge gave her half his reduced pension, their paid-for modest but comfortable home, the family car, and restored her maiden name. Their daughter, herself twice-divorced and mired in therapy, sided completely with her mother in the unpleasant recriminations mounted by both her parents.

And suddenly—the timing seemed calculated by some higher power to Zilligen—he began to feel the inexorable effects of aging. Out of the blue, his bowels fluctuated between explosive diarrhea and days-long sieges of painful constipation. Most of his remaining teeth ached dully at the roots. His joints stiffened, his breathing deteriorated, unpredictable fits of wheezing interrupted by phlegmy coughing, though he hadn't smoked in a decade. His feet were cold and clammy in all weathers. Balls of pain flared randomly, deep in his guts. His skin dried and flaked, his whiskers turned white as snow, his once-bushy head of hair thinned to expose glints of shiny scalp, mottled with blotches. When he walked too fast, his vision blurred and swam, and when he stood in place to clear his eyes, dizziness flashed in his skull.

So is this it? Zilligen wondered. *It.* Not just yet, he thought, but knew better than to hope for recovery, rejuvenation. His clock ticking louder and faster by the hour—so it felt—he needed, *wanted* some insights, if not answers.

So he made it through two days, passing Madam Auchmunty's house, the crude sign, but never stopped to look or read, afraid he'd lose control, rush up her walk, ring her bell, be turned away for failing to give her her ponder-time, afraid she'd cite this as an example of how not-nice a man he was. I think, Zilligen repeated like a mantra, I'm at least average in terms of niceness!

She was waiting for him. He was sure he did not ring her bell, fingertip only poised to do so when her door popped open with a crunching sound, Madam Auchmunty standing aside for Zilligen to enter. She wore the same housecoat, silver-shot hair in the same clipped bun—somehow he'd expected her to dress up a little for the occasion, as he had. He followed her to the cluttered living room, smelled the same thick cooking smell, sat at her silent direction on the sofa that whooshed and sank under him, faced her.

"Yes," she said, and, "I have pondered you, Mr. Zilligen."

"You can call me Augie," he said, tried to smile.

"With some . . . reservation, and after some hesitation," she said as if he had not spoken, "I have concluded it is suitable to assist you. Your situation is rather dire."

"I'm accepted as a client?"

"Yes," Madam Auchmunty said. He half-smiled, shrugged his shoulders, squirmed on the sofa's cushions, waited for her to say more.

When she did not, he said, "I guess I should ask your rates? I'm not exactly flush."

"My honorarium," she said, "is one hundred dollars per session. Cash."

"Oh," Zilligen said, and, "That's a reach for me," and, "I don't carry that kind of money on me as a rule," and, "How many sessions? How long's a session?" He had visions of hundred-dollar bills flying around the room like a swarm of bees, a rushing sound of high wind, heat in his armpits and groin as he struggled to recall numbers, his monthly income, his checking and small savings account balances, the total of his monthly bills—heat, light, water, and sewage, rent, groceries, pocket money.

"You *can* afford it. *If* you're serious," she said.

Zilligen closed his eyes, took a deep breath, held it a beat, exhaled loudly, said, "Does the last time count as one session?"

He felt no relief when Madam Auchmunty smiled, a big broad smile revealing her bad teeth, shook her head no. He felt better when she said, "Nor is today a . . . *session*. Today," she said, "I convey my willingness to proceed with you, and my terms. Having just done so, I now convey the mode I have elected as appropriate. We shall be engaged with voices," she said, sat back a little in her chair.

"Voices?"

"Voices."

"What *voices*? Whose?" Zilligen said.

Madam Auchmunty said, "Which, who, is not up to me to determine. When we begin—*not* today—I will speak to you, but it will not be me you hear. You will hear voices, the voices of such people as come forth through me to address you."

Zilligen thought about it while she watched him, searching for the right questions to put, the right way to put them. "Yes?" she said when he did not speak.

He was able to say, "You're saying, like, you talk to me, but it's somebody else, you don't know who? It could be anybody? Do they, like, inhabit your body or something? I'm lost here." She smiled again, less broadly.

"Mr. Zilligen," she said, seeming not to hear him invite her again to call him Augie, "be assured they will be the voices of people you know well, who know *you* well! They will speak from a vantage superior to ours. They are empowered to address the issues which concern you."

"How's that?" he said. "What . . . *vantage*?"

Madam Auchmunty said, no longer smiling, "They are people who have left us. Passed away. They are *dead* people, Mr. Zilligen."

"You talk to the dead?" he said, almost laughed. Zilligen decided to call it off, stand, leave—this creepy old bag, he thought, is either a con or she's wackier than I am!

"No," Madam Auchmunty said. "They talk *through* me. To *you.*"

"This sounds, pardon me for saying, but I should be honest—"

"Indeed you should," she interrupted, but he went on.

"—this sounds like so much mumbo-jumbo, you know?" She smiled again now, emitted a short cackle.

"Suppose you wait and see what you think after we've begun, Mr. Zilligen?" He leaned forward.

"You couldn't give me a little sample just now here?"

She said, "I will not. Come in two days. I guarantee you will not be disappointed in that regard. Go now."

"Do you go into some kind of trance?" he asked as he followed her to the door.

"No, Mr. Zilligen," she said, opened the door, "I do not."

"Hey," he said, put his hand on the door to prevent her shutting it, "you can feel free to call me Augie, you know. Mr. Zilligen's kind of formal. We could use first names here."

"No," she said, and, "I would not be at all comfortable with that. As I said before, you're not a nice man, are you, Mr. Zilligen," and closed the door.

On the sidewalk, he felt again a mixture of emotions—thrilled, shamed, angry at her obnoxious, opaque manner, the snub. And Zilligen wondered how he'd kill the two days standing between him and what he wanted, needed.

He killed the time guessing at the dead who would speak to him through Madam Auchmunty. When he thought about it, there weren't many who came to mind—not many he thought knew him at all well. His parents were gone—what, his father twenty-nine years, his mother only a couple years after. The possibility he might hear them brought tears, a choking in his throat. It was logical it would be his parents—who knew him better? Zilligen put his money on it being his mother and father, lost himself sometimes for hours while his television droned and day melted into night at his apartment windows, recalling them. They'd been good parents, he a good son, he felt certain of that. If anybody knew him well, it was them; they'd seen him go from child to boy to man, loved him. Zilligen let himself weep, remembering his parents' love, his love for them he seemed to have forgotten long ago. Oh, he hoped it would be his parents' voices!

And there was his baby sister Rosemary, taken when she was only nine by the plague of bulbar polio the vaccine hadn't yet been invented to prevent. She was just a child, but surely she'd loved him! And the grief and gloom that settled on his parents, his home, his childhood self, dried his tears, this memory stopping him like a sudden paralysis striking him in the dark of his apartment, where he sat, immobile, long into the night.

If Madam Auchmunty brought him his long-dead baby sister's voice, would she still be a child, or did she grow up, age as he had, and if this happened to the dead, would Zilligen recognize her voice? Could he even remember Rosemary's nine-year-old voice? Then he remembered the sound of his sister wailing as the polio forced her head backwards, rolled her eyes up into her head, closed her lungs, and he wept again, heaved and wailed as she had, and it was near morning of a new day before that passed, left him free to guess at other possibilities.

Auntie Flo, his mother's sister, her husband Uncle Buzz—not too likely because they moved to another state when Zilligen was nineteen, in the army in Japan, and he never saw them again, didn't attend their funerals. He could muster no memory of them save one Thanksgiving when they all—Flo, Buzz, his parents, Rosemary—sat together at the table, Uncle Buzz giving a quick, mumbled grace. He couldn't remember whose house they gathered at, the specific year. No, Zilligen thought, the aunt and uncle, childless, were improbable. And he was relieved thinking of them brought no tears, no tangible gloom, certainly no grief.

Who else?

Zilligen had fleeting thoughts about such dead as he had known, but names, faces, memories of any dimension or texture eluded him, like the dreams he knew he dreamed dozing in and out of true sleep as he waited for time to pass, *real* in some way, but beyond hope of recollection. It would have been better, he thought, to have taken more long walks, walked himself numb. He killed the two days Madam Auchmunty required, but they were agony for him, left him desperate with anticipation and anxiety when he reached her door for the first session with voices she said she had no control over.

It was the same, unkempt, the odor—soup simmering on the stove?—her housecoat and ragged bun clipped at her neck. She said, "Sit," without pointing at the sofa, took a chair. "Are you prepared to be receptive?" she asked.

Zilligen, lips and tongue and throat dry, managed to say, "I think so. What's going to happen here, exactly?" Five crisp twenty-dollar bills burned in his pocket.

Madam Auchmunty said, "I will appear to be speaking, but you will hear another's voice. Pay attention."

"Whose?" he said.

"I have no idea," she said. "The possibilities are virtually endless. You've lived a long time, Mr. Zilligen. Hundreds, thousands have died around and about you."

"I guess I wasn't aware," he said. "Can I talk back?"

"Probably. I imagine you can pose questions. Be sensitive to context," she said.

"So," Zilligen said, and, "So let's go then?" They were silent a moment, and then Madam Auchmunty closed her eyes—Oh ho! he thought, hokum! Then her lips moved, she spoke, but it was not her voice. This voice was male—a boy's, and Zilligen did not recognize it at first, thought, so she can do false voices! But there was something wrong. Her lips moved as if she spoke softly, slowly, but the voice was loud, almost shouting at him.

The voice said, "I'll be dipped! I will be dipped in shit and call me chocolate!" It said, "I can't hardly believe it! Of all people in all the world. Looky, looky here!" Zilligen wanted to ask who this was, ask Madam Auchmunty, but she sat still as stone, only moving her lips, didn't seem to be breathing, not hearing the voice. Then the voice said, "Little Augie Z.! Don't you know me, Aug?"

"Who are you?" Zilligen heard himself say. "Who is this?"

"Here's a hint," it said, and, "Diving off the dock out at that lake beach, the private one we're not allowed to swim? Second hint. You paddled out over your head, those water-wing things you wore to float you 'cause you don't swim so good, huh? *Get wet!* you yelled at me. So I dove off the dock like I knew what the hell I was doing. Still don't know me, Augie Z.?"

Zilligen knew the voice, said, "Paulie Hunt!"

"Give that man a cee-gar!" Paulie Hunt said.

"Paulie," he said, sat forward, spoke loud and fast, didn't see Madam Auchmunty, her slowly moving lips, saw the memory of Paulie Hunt, the private beach, paddling in his water-wings out over his head, Paulie charging to the end of the pier, diving. He said, "Paulie, you dove into shallow water, you broke your neck, you were in an iron lung the rest of your life!"

"Right again!" Paulie Hunt said.

"I visited you once in the hospital, you had a mirror up over your face so people could see your face without standing up beside you, the iron lung clanked, you smiled the whole time I visited!"

Paulie Hunt said, "You visited me just the once because you couldn't take it. You felt *guilty* for telling me come on in and get wet. I never saw you again, Augie Z.! You don't even know when I died, you dumb jerk!"

"Nobody told me!" Zilligen said. "I was ten, eleven. I was only a little kid, Paulie!"

"Come off it!" Paulie Hunt said, and said, "So tell me what you learned from it, Aug."

He said, "I never ever again went swimming in my life! I wouldn't let my daughter take swimming lessons at the Y when she wanted to. I've been scared of bodies of water ever since!"

The voice laughed, an ugly, sarcastic laugh, said, "That's you, Augie the Z., never learned a thing about anything, did you! You're as dumb now as you were then, you dumb-ass! Get wise to yourself, Augie. And no hard feelings here," Paulie Hunt said, and spoke no more.

Zilligen had no idea how long the silence lasted. It was a long silence, and then he was looking at Madam Auchmunty, her eyes now open, blank behind her spectacles, and he felt no strength in his body, as if he were hollow, felt sweat on his face, his hands locked together in his lap.

"Yes," she said, her voice.

"He's gone?" Zilligen said.

"Yes."

"Can he come back? Some other time?"

"He will not."

"He called me dumb. It was Paulie Hunt. He broke his neck diving off a pier. I visited him in his iron lung. Why's he come talk to me? I don't think I'm dumber than average," Zilligen said.

"That's for *you* to ponder," Madam Auchmunty said. She stood, told him to go, stopped him at the door, held out her hand. He fished the new twenties from his pocket, handed them over.

"How long do I have to wait for the next?" he asked.

"Tomorrow," she said, "if it suits you."

"It wasn't very long for a hundred bucks," he said.

"We're not on the clock here, Mr. Zilligen," she said.

"He called me Augie Z. All my pals when I was a kid called me that," he said.

She said, "I hope that's a comfort to you, Mr. Zilligen," and nudged him out the door, closed it hard after him.

Zilligen spent the night rerunning what Paulie Hunt said, arguing with the boy's ghost, telling him he never meant Paulie should go head first off that pier when he yelled at him to come on in and get wet, explaining he did not visit him after the first time because he just couldn't stand to look at his sickly smiling face in that mirror stuck up on the iron lung, forming and reforming things he wished he had said to Paulie—*I was a little kid, Paulie. If somebody ever told me when you died I'd have gone to your funeral. I'm sorry for what happened to you, Paulie, but a person's life goes on, they forget things, don't think about things. And I'm not so ignorant as you say, I read the paper, I watch TV news twice a night, I've read a few books, you know!*

He feared he would not be able to sleep, but he did, feared if he did he would have bad dreams, and he did dream, but it was a good dream, something vague about his sister and his daughter, both happy little kids together alive at the same time in the dream, Zilligen happy with them.

This time he handed Madam Auchmunty two fifties, said, "This is going to tap me out if we go on too long at this."

She took his money, held it in her hand throughout the second session, when Buddy Rumsey spoke to him through her. Zilligen had been hoping for his parents, his sister Rosemary, even Auntie Flo or Uncle Buzz.

Buddy Rumsey said through Madam Auchmunty's barely moving lips, "Hello there, Augie," and Zilligen recognized him at once.

He said, "You're Buddy Rumsey! We were bunkmates at Eta Jima Barracks! You got shot in the head and killed by some Jap, you were banging his wife and he snuck up on you and shot you in the head right while you were doing it! I went to the memorial service they had in the post chapel! I remember thinking I couldn't really believe you were killed, we were best buddies nearly a year over there!" When Buddy Rumsey said nothing to this, Zilligen said, "I was terribly sorry you were killed so young that way, Buddy."

Buddy said, "Easy for you to say, especially now, Augie."

"I was a good friend to you, Buddy," he said.

"You couldn't," Buddy said, "have cared a rat's ass less, Augie. All you cared about was goldbricking on the job, getting sloshed on cheap Jap beer, getting laid as much as you could. Which was not all that often, I've got to say." Zilligen looked closely at Madam Auchmunty before he spoke, wondered if she heard what she said, but there was nothing either way showing on her face, her lips quivering a little.

He said, "I was so young, Buddy, it's normal to sow your oats at that age, isn't it? You did the same."

Buddy Rumsey said, "I didn't get the chance to begin to do any different, did I? You did, Augie, but you flubbed the dub right up to this very minute."

"I don't get you," Zilligen said, and, "I got mature after I got discharged. I went to college for an associate's degree in econ, I got a decent job, married, had my family until it all went to hell on me. You don't have a right to say I'm the same as then!"

Buddy Rumsey's voice had a sudden edge in it. "Knock off the bullshit, Augie!" he said. "So you only drank on occasion and learned to keep your pecker in your pants, you were a for-shit student in school, you're lucky you graduated! The point is you've never cared a crap for anyone but your damn self!"

"Not true!" Zilligen said, believed.

"Your wife and daughter for example," Buddy said.

"What about them? I treated them well."

"You never gave a shit, basically," Buddy said. "You were just too scared to do anything open, but you've never given the least shit, truly, about anyone, face it."

"I liked you as my best friend in life then, Bud," he said, felt like he might start crying, but that passed.

"So where were you, friend, when that Jap Papa-san fucker blew my brains out my forehead?"

"I think I was out on the strip boozing with some guys I knew in QM, Buddy," he said. "How should I know you had some married Mama-san you were banging? I'm to blame you got killed?"

Buddy Rumsey laughed loud through Madam Auchmunty's lips, said, "You're only to blame for your stupid self, Augie."

"Me?"

"That's the fact, Jack!" Buddy said.

"How's that, for Christ's sake? Tell me how that works, please?" But Buddy Rumsey did not speak again, and Zilligen looked into Madam Auchmunty's opened eyes. He said, "He's gone already?"

She said, "He's been *gone* for years. You know that, Mr. Zilligen."

At the door, he turned to her, said, "Are you hearing what's said in there as we're saying it?"

She smiled, not a nice smile, said, "Don't be embarrassed. There's very little language or anything else I haven't heard well before you came to me."

Relieved, Zilligen said, "Are you sure you can't hook up with, say, my folks or my little sister who died very young from polio?" She shook her head, still smiling that not-nice smile, holding his two fifties. "Just to get it off my chest, I am not a person that doesn't care for anyone but himself, OK?"

"So you say, Mr. Zilligen," she said, not smiling at all. "Tomorrow?" she said.

He looked at the money in her hand and said, "I'm just wondering how long I can afford this."

She said, "You'll know when you need to, Mr. Zilligen," and closed the door in his face.

Zilligen slept well that night, convinced Buddy Rumsey was wrong about him—he was *not* an uncaring person! Drifting into dreamless slumber, he was soothed by the certainty the voice he heard tomorrow would have to have better things to say of him. There was some good in everyone, wasn't there?

When Madam Auchmunty opened the door to him late the following morning, he handed her a hundred-dollar bill, shivering at the thought of his shrinking savings account, said, "I'm really hoping for something more useful here today, you know? I mean, it's a lot of money down the drain just to be told you're dumb and totally self-centered, don't you think?"

She said, "Truth is more often than not very hard to accept, Mr. Zilligen."

"The truth's got to be the whole truth. It'd be nice if I'd maybe get just a little consideration for having maybe a few good qualities too, huh?" he said.

She said, "Shall we sit down and find out?"

Seated across from her on the sofa, he watched her eyes shut, lips begin to slowly move, and recognized the voice at once.

This voice said, "I'm glad to be with you, Mr. Zilligen. August. How strange to be able to call you *August* at last! Hello, August," and there was a lilt of girlish laughter.

"Margaret Schumacher! Maggie!" Zilligen said, and, "I never called you Maggie all those years at the office, I just used to think of you as *Maggie,* which I hope you'll forgive if it's disrespectful. Margaret, jeez, you only died, what was it? Three years back? Kidney failure. You got a transplant but it didn't work, from your twin sister I heard it was, but it rejected and you died! We took up a collection for a floral tribute all through the building. I wanted to come to your funeral, but circumstances didn't allow," he said. He was surprised at the energy, the excitement in his voice, how he smiled as he spoke. "They downsized me, Maggie, cut into my pension, didn't throw me a dinner, no gold watch, no nothing," he added.

Margaret Schumacher said, "You also called me other things you never said out loud. *Maggie Tits* was one. You thought what a terrific lay I'd make, August. You liked to fantasize a lot about sleeping with me, what it would be like to wake up in bed beside me and wake me up with kisses and then we'd do it again. Oh, August!" she said, and there was a sound like a sob.

Zilligen, stunned, smile wiped off his face, needed several seconds before he could speak. When he did, his voice was a thin croak. "You knew my *thoughts*? Or you only know them now? Jeez, Margaret, I apologize for being offensive, I never meant anything serious by anything I thought!" Now it was obvious Margaret Schumacher was crying as she spoke, sniffling, pausing to swallow, her voice breaking. Zilligan was ashamed of himself, embarrassed for her, barely able to believe what she told him.

She said, "Oh August! It is *so* pathetic! I loved you, August, and I tried in so many little ways to make you know that! *I* thought about sleeping with *you!* I sensed how you felt about me, I felt the same, but you never responded, so many times you could have said something, it would have happened, August. But you wouldn't let it. Do you know why you were like that, August?"

He checked to make sure Madam Auchmunty's eyes were still shut, Margaret still there to hear him, took a breath, said, "It was just dirty thoughts I had about you, Maggie. I think I even knew somehow I could have made a move, but I was afraid of getting tangled up in something like that. Jeez, I was a married man, I had a grown daughter with all kinds of problems, I just didn't have it in me to pull something like that off, see? It's sad, I know. If it was now, I swear I would. My wife divorced me, my daughter's got no use for me, I'd go for it in a minute if you were still around." He waited for her to say something, but there was only Margaret Schumacher's unbroken weeping coming through Madam Auchmunty's lips.

He said, "I guess maybe I passed on an opportunity. OK. I thought dirty thoughts. I did think of you as Maggie Tits and some other stuff. But I never meant to hurt you, Maggie. I swear."

Her weeping slowed, ended, she coughed, said, "What kept you away from my funeral, do you think, August?" He writhed on Madam Auchmunty's sofa.

Zilligen said, "I didn't want the complications. I'm not a funeral-goer, you probably know since you know everything else, looks like. If I went the wife'd wonder why, things were pretty strained for us. This is just before she split from me and took everything I had in the bargain. I didn't want complications, it was easiest and best for me just to put it out of mind, see?"

"August," she said, and he waited, but she said no more. When he looked into Madam Auchmunty's eyes, there was something different in her expression. Zilligan looked away, fumbled for his handkerchief, blew his nose, stood up.

She remained in her chair, said, "You're really a worse person than I originally perceived, Mr. Zilligen."

He stumbled toward the door, said, "I'm paying good money looking for some insights, all I get's indicted instead."

"Perhaps," she said, "the *indictment,* as you call it, is your answer," and followed him out of her living room.

"That's your take on it," he said, and, "Bring me somebody doesn't have an axe to grind's got my name on it. Where's my folks? Where's my baby sister died so young? I'm wasting my time here, besides blowing money I don't have."

"Perhaps," she said as she opened the door, stepped onto her porch, "they don't wish to say anything to you. Perhaps they have just enough regard for you to spare you what they'd have to say?"

"You won't catch me coming back," Zilligen said as he went down the steps.

"That's a wise decision, Mr. Zilligen," she said, "if you can stand by it."

"Watch me!" he shouted from the sidewalk.

"I do!" she called back to him, shut her door.

Zilligen endured several hard days and nights. He stayed mornings in his one-bedroom efficiency, killed time and distracted himself preparing elaborate breakfasts he had no appetite for, watching the tube's stupid talk shows, repetitious coverage of natural disasters, brushfire wars, famine, and political and celebrity scandals. After lunches he tried to force down, he had to get out to keep from talking to the walls, so he walked. He walked long and far—always skirted Madam Auchmunty's neighborhood—walked hoping to avoid rehashing the previous night's dreams.

They infuriated him because they were good dreams, happy. He dreamed about his parents, miraculously never having died, there with him as he was now, his present age. He dreamed of his little sister Rosemary, she was grown up, looked different, but he knew it was her. He dreamed once of Paulie Hunt, not in an iron lung, but sitting up in a chair, as old as Zilligen, quite alive, still Zilligen's good boyhood pal from way back. He dreamed of Buddy Rumsey, who still wore his uniform— Buddy was in some dangerous place, though there were no Japs there, no Papa-san with a pistol, and Zilligen took him by the arm, led him somewhere safe where they drank enormous mugs of cold beer. He even dreamed of his ex-wife and troubled daughter, his wife still seeming to care for him, about him, his daughter a very happy girl with no need for medication for her mood swings. He had many short dreams about Margaret Schumacher.

They were joyous snippets, Zilligen and Maggie in places they'd never been, in a park or woods, in a car, holding hands on a walk somewhere. Zilligen was both young and old in these short dreams that always woke him, but Maggie was younger than he'd ever known her, more lively, lovelier by far than she was in life, flirting with him. But they never did anything, no sex in these dreams, even though it was clear he wanted it, could have it if he asked, so they woke him to frustration and anger and shame and guilt, which didn't seem fair to Zilligen.

And though his walking tired him, helped him sleep nights, and his dreams gave him brief joy, that they were only dreams became a weight he knew he could not continue to bear each afternoon through the city. So he cleaned out his savings account, closed it, and went to Madam Auchmunty's with a roll of bills bulging his pocket, a hard knot against his thigh.

Her house looked the same, the sign propped up against the porch, the palm like a policeman's stopping traffic, unmown grass, stunted shrubs, but somehow it felt a little different, like the dream of a house he knew, not a real house. Yet it was real, the creaking steps, the porch floorboards moaning under him, windows blocked by curtains. Zilligen put his hand in his pocket, gripped his money like a rock picked up for throwing, pushed her bell with the forefinger of his free hand.

He pushed and pushed, leaned his body into it. There was no ring or buzz, no sound of movement inside, window curtains still as the air around him. He then began to knock, to pound on the door, and still nothing but the noise of his pounding, his sore fist. Then he began to shout her name.

He shouted, screamed until he was hoarse, breathless. He called her name, told her how much money he carried, yelled that there had to be others, the dead who knew him, who could tell him things about himself he so wanted, needed to know. He pleaded, begged, and when this yielded nothing, he raged, called her fake, fraud, huckster, phoney.

He stopped only when exhausted, barely able to stand without swaying there on Madam Auchmunty's porch. He knew she was behind her door, knew she would never open it to him again—she thought him despicable, unworthy. Zilligen, giddy from his effort, turned away, went down her steps, reached the sidewalk not certain he had it in him to walk, walk to his apartment, walk anywhere, but even as he whimpered he set forth, one foot in front of the other, remembering how the longest journey began with the shortest step, and was surprised to find some comfort and strength, if only a little, in the certainty that, when he died, he would know everything.

The Emancipation of Hoytie Rademacher

. . . I will not let thee go, except thou bless me.

—Genesis 32:26

Right on first sight, I didn't like Ft. Myers Beach, Florida. I still don't. First sight, I semi-wished I was still back in my rat-trap San Francisco apartment, facing up to the music, semi-wished I hadn't driven cross-country in the hope of my mother saving my bacon one more time. But only half-wished.

I didn't like the Florida heat, which was extra-oppressive because of the dampness coming off the Gulf. The air smelled like old fish to me, and the bright sun burning overhead, reflecting off everything, stung my eyes, made me squint, which gives me a dull headache that never goes away.

And even in my behind-on-the-payments Lexus, I didn't feel I fit in with all the Cadillacs and Lincolns and SUVs and limos whizzing by me. I didn't like the people I saw, all these *old* people dressed in colors I wouldn't be seen dead in. Fat women with opaque sunglasses and flowing tents for dresses. And dried up old ladies with dyed hair and too much lipstick and jewelry. And old men in shorts showing their toothpick legs.

Nor did I like the greenery, so bright it also hurt my eyes, all those palms and spiked plants, the golf course communities strung out along the four-lane streets, and apartments and condos with names like *villa*-this and *shores*-that. Not to mention all the little tourist trap shops hawking T-shirts and seashells and beachwear and plastic flamingoes and gazing balls. And a lot of construction everywhere raising sandy dust that got pasted to my skin once I got out of my ripe-to-be-repossessed Lexus.

There's something sickly about it all, a place I would never have contemplated relocating in a new life.

I hit Ft. Myers Beach mid-morning, and, candidly, looking a mess. I needed to look as good as I could for my mother, so I employed a gas station restroom thick with lavatory smells to change into something respectable and wash up. I gave myself a whore-bath in the sink, shaved, nicking myself so I bled, patched my chin with a hunk of toilet paper, which I remembered to remove before I got out of my Lexus in the parking area of my mother's complex, which was named Seaside Vistas.

Seaside Vistas was just another of the sugar-cube white high-rises lining the beach as far as I could see in either direction. With the sun bouncing off them, it was blinding to look up, try to see where her apartment was in all the rows of windows and balconies, winking like diamond chips in the sunlight. The grounds were all barbered green, dotted with tennis courts where nobody played tennis in that heat, a big pool with a cabana where nobody swam, dotted with floral plots in carnival colors, stands of fat-trunk palms, spiked plants in bunches. Just in the walk from visitor parking to the big glass and brass entrance, I broke a hard sweat, felt in my armpits and crotch like I wore hot-packs.

The entrance lobby was a relief, air-conditioned chill, and quiet as a church after the sound of traffic and the surf in the background outside. My mother, I could tell from Seaside Vistas, the barbered grounds, the lobby all wood and glass and plush carpet, was clearly still in the bucks, giving me real hope as I stood there trying to let the cold air dry me.

I pressed the silver button under her name engraved on a silver plate—
Lucille H. Addison. #605. My mother reverted to her maiden name when
she took me and left my father, back when I was aged seven. She wanted
to have a fresh slate for the new life she set out on. A stippled bronze
mailbox also had her name on it on a printed card. I pressed the button
twice, waited, feeling just a little sinking feeling—what if my mother
wasn't home at this hour? But she was.

"Yes," she said, her firm, clear woman's voice a little metallic over the
intercom.

I said, "Mommy? It's me. Hoytie. I'm here."

All she said was, "Yes," again, and then the door to the inside lobby
buzzed like a loud snooze alarm, and I pushed in, found my way to the
elevator. The inner lobby was as chilled as the entranceway, dark with
indirect lighting. I had to adjust to the dimness, like somebody coming
out of a snowstorm. The elevator doors slid open the instant I hit *Up,*
and I rode up six floors, the elevator all dark wood paneling, only a distant humming as it shot up fast. And there I was in front of her door,
a brass and ceramic knocker on it that rang chimes when I lifted it to
knock.

It wasn't the way I wanted or planned. I wanted to look good, but
didn't. I had a bad shave, a restroom whore-bath. I was sweated to where
my shirt and shorts were plastered to me, my feet on fire in my shoes,
which could have used a shine, my tie off-center, wings of my shirt collar curled. And I could feel little twitches of flatulence in my gut wanting out, which I had to hold in. I was suddenly thinking why it was I
neglected to bring my mother something, flowers or a bottle of decent
wine? So I wasn't so hopeful when she opened the door and stood back
for me to come in.

"Hi, Mommy," I said.

"Hello, Hoyt," is what she said, turned and walked into her living room,
me following.

"You look wonderful, Mommy," I said. She did. When she was young,
my childhood and youth days, my mother was a certified stunner. I remembered how men took a second look when we walked down a street

or through a store, in a restaurant. When I was very young, seven, eight, nine, I didn't get it. Later, a teen, when I'd be home with her on vacation or a semester break from Wayland Academy, where she sent me to board, I remember I was proud of the way she caught men's eyes. Later, at college, Ripon College—where I dropped out due to poor grades what should have been my senior year—I was maybe a little envious of how people gave her the once-over, perhaps wanted that attention for myself?

And here she was, age seventy-six, still great looking. Her blonde hair, which I inherited, was silvery, but thick and full, styled really nice. Her skin was still good, kind of a soft glow to her face and bare arms, her hands. She used some cosmetics, but not too much, the way some old women trying to hold onto it will. Her lips and long nails matched a soft red-pink, and her toenails, which I could see because of the open-toe slippers she wore, also matched. Her dress was what's called a dressing gown, I think, like she hadn't been up long, about ready to dress for the day. Her dress was long and filmy, sheer, flowered, but not garish, with tasteful, muted colors. She wore several rings, but not too many, and bracelets on both arms that tinkled like tiny bells when she moved, and a brushed gold necklace. Seventy-six years aged, my mother would, I could see, still catch people's eyes. "You really do look great," I said.

"I take care of myself, Hoyt," she said, and what made me feel bad, added, "You could do with a little of that."

"I'm out of shape some," I said, "but I feel pretty fit." Which was of course a lie, but what else could I say? I tried to give her a little hug and kiss hello; she didn't lean back away from me, but I only got in a little dry kiss on her cheek. Her cheek felt cool and smooth to my lips, her scent a very subtle sort of floral with coconut.

"Well, sit down, Hoyt," she said. Which I did. I was half-hoping she'd offer me something, coffee, brunch, a drink if I was lucky. She didn't. I took out my Camels, looked around for an ashtray. She said, "Thank you for not smoking, Hoyt. If you must, you can go out on the balcony." Through the patio doors I could see the Gulf stretching off forever.

"So," I said, not at all ready or primed to start talking turkey to her. "I guess we have a lot of catching up to do. How long has it been, Mommy? Four years?"

"Nearly six," she said. "Since I moved south."

"Oh. Right you are. So. Tell me all about your life and all here, Mommy." It was, I could see from where I sat across a large coffee table from her, a very posh apartment. How many bedrooms? I flashed on my San Francisco digs, which were distinctly seedy, took in her Seaside Vistas apartment, had a quick thought about how two people could live here with room to spare—but I wasn't about to touch that one unless push came to shove.

"I live," my mother said, "a very orderly and quite routine existence I find wholly satisfying." And then she told me about her activities there in Seaside Vistas, Ft. Myers Beach, Florida.

She told me, like she was interviewing for a job I could give her, or as if I was a reporter doing on article on her—like I was a stranger.

In passing, I will confess that, except for assistance with various ventures and marital problems she provided me, I had not kept up with my mother's life very well.

She told me about the fitness club she belonged to, aerobics and swimming and such, her and some of her Seaside Vistas friends, both men and women fellow-retirees. Three times a week. She played both golf and tennis, but was not obsessive over either, unlike some of her *crowd*, as she called her friends. She had a public library card, read a lot, mostly histories and biographies of famous personages in history. She belonged to a gourmet group, her crowd again, where they had monthly dinner parties, each person bringing a dish according to the theme of the dinner. She had a symphony subscription. She only watched television for the weather forecasts, hated talk shows—"All those complaining women and amoral celebrities," she said. She swam laps in the Seaside Vistas pool. She watched her stocks on the Internet.

It got me wondering if maybe my mother had a boyfriend, even at her age, in that crowd of hers she told me about. But I wasn't about to touch that one, even curious as I was, and wondering how I'd feel about it if she did have a boyfriend.

I said, "You've got a computer, Mommy? I'm alien to those things."

"They're simple enough if you apply yourself, Hoyt," she answered me.

"You'll have to show me on yours," I said. Which she didn't respond to. Then, when she finally asked to hear about my life, which I knew was coming, and dreaded, I said, "Mommy, I really could use a smoke. Can I burn one on your balcony?"

"If you absolutely can't refrain," she said, and had to show me how to work the latch on the patio doors. Out on the balcony, groping in my mind for a strategy, I watched her disappear somewhere out of the living room. Then I was alone on the balcony, six floors up.

I smoked two Camels, and did some thinking. The heat and humidity weren't so bad up there where some sea air moved, and it was impressive, the Gulf stretching out forever, waves winking in the sun, cloudless, some gulls and other assorted seabirds flying past. A good place for serious thinking.

What I thought about was my life, compared to my mother's. I didn't have any activities or interests, unless I counted the hassle of my most recent unsuccessful venture and the bust-up of my third marriage, Marlene. In San Francisco, I had mostly stayed in my digs in recent months, smoking Camels and imbibing a deal more of the strong stuff than was good for me. I ate out, fast-food junk mostly, and squatted in front of the tube.

For a second I thought I was going to lose it, bawl. How was it my mother seemed to have this great, full life with a crowd of friends and wholesome recreational and cultural activities, and Hoytie Rademacher had bad debt and failed relationships and precarious health? How did this all come to pass? What frustrated me, made me want to weep, was I couldn't see how I got this way. Where had fifty-plus years, half a century, gone? It was like I was once seven, back in Wisconsin, with a father and mother I loved, who loved me, and then, *zap!* I was fifty-plus with my life gone down the porcelain convenience. Did I just somehow magically blink?

But I finished my second Camel, looked out at the Gulf until my eyes cleared, looked back inside my mother's apartment, and there she was on her sofa again, and I had to go back inside. But a little hope came to me as I slid the patio door open and stepped in. She had come through for me before, possibly would again—and also I felt a tickle of guilt, relating to how Hoytie Rademacher was his mother's sole heir. Though she was in such great shape, the odds against my outliving her were long. That eased my guilt tickle.

"Tell me what is it this time, Hoyt?" she asked me right off the bat.

"Mommy . . ." is all I said, trying to think on my feet how to tell her.

Before I could come up with anything, she said, "Could you possibly address me as something other than *Mommy,* Hoyt? Even *Mom* would be preferable."

"But you're my *mommy!*" I said, and then I did lose it. What I said to her had to come through my tears and sniffling, blowing my nose, coughing. I said, "I'm in some hot water, Mommy, and I need your help! Your Hoytie's in kind of a jam, and you're the only one can help me!" For what felt like a long time she didn't say anything. I could hear my wheezing, rattled breathing, trying to get control, and I heard her sigh hard several times, like she had to get *her* breath, muster her words before she could speak.

She said, "Are you having trouble with what's-her-name, this one, Marlene?"

"That too," I said. "I mean, we're splitting the blanket, except I don't have a blanket to speak of to split." She sighed hard again.

"Besides *that too,* what else, Hoyt?" I didn't like the way my mother looked at me from behind her glasses, like I was a stranger off the street, like one of the panhandling street homeless who accost passersby in San Francisco.

"I made some unfortunate investments."

"I won't ask for particulars this time."

"I just need to sort of gather myself, Mommy, get back on my feet and start swinging again, as it were."

What she told me, and it truly hurt me to hear it, was, "Not this time, Hoyt! Not a penny. I've given and I've given, and I'll give no more. Reach for your bootstraps, Hoyt!"

At which I again lost it, broke down there in her Seaside Vistas apartment, weeping so hard I shook like I was freezing to death. And my mother didn't move an inch from where she sat across the coffee table from me, didn't comfort me in any fashion, just sat there and watched me fall apart. I was convinced my life was over for good this time, age fifty-plus.

It's a documented fact my mother provided me significant assistance over the years, on exactly five occasions. Of course, each time she was less pleased to do so. Each time she said it was the last. But it never was.

Twice it was in the shambles of terminating my first two marriages. The first was Billie Frechette, who I married just shortly after I left Ripon College in what should have been my senior year. Billie Frechette took just about all I had in her divorce, so I had to go to my mother for some start-up funds, get going again, being emotionally distressed and all. But I had a lot of self-confidence in those days, back up in Wisconsin, and she was making money hand over fist selling real estate in Milwaukee. She always got featured in realty news articles and ads for being a multimillion-dollar seller. So she didn't seem to balk when I went to her for help. The worst she said to me that time was, "That marriage was doomed from the get-go, Hoyt. I'll have you know you disappointed me grievously, leaving school, Hoyt, and I made no bones about my feelings about you marrying that girl."

"I was in love with her when I married her, Mommy," I said. She sort of snorted at that, but she did provide me the funds I needed to start anew.

When I experienced my second divorce, which is when I had relocated to Tulsa, Oklahoma, tired of Wisconsin winters, I made a special trip up to Milwaukee to see her. Opal Dideaux made her divorce from me very unpleasant, and I still have some liabilities with respect to her, but she's long since moved to Arizona, so would play hell trying to collect from there, as a lawyer informed me. At this divorce, my mother said to me, "There are some people just aren't suited to matrimony, Hoyt. Thank God or whoever you've not sired any offspring."

I said, "Maybe I'm like you in that respect, Mommy, ill-suited for marriage."

"Your father," she said to me, "was the one ill-suited. But you'll note I haven't replicated that episode in my life."

"But you produced a child, Mommy," I said. "Me."

"Let's hope," she said, "you don't make me rue the day." And she did bail me out of most of the fallout of that divorce, though I could tell she didn't like it one bit. But, as I said, she was coining money in realty sales there in Milwaukee.

The remaining three instances in which she provided me assistance had to do with the worst three, the least successful, of my financial ventures. I am the first to confess what I did *not* inherit from my mother: sound business sense. Though the blame in all fairness has to be shared with the various associates I was involved with in these ventures, some of them just inept, some untrustworthy.

The first such venture, when I was still in Oklahoma—though not in Tulsa, having relocated to Ardmore, a much smaller community—had to do with oil and natural gas exploration. She said to me, "Did I give birth to an utter dunce, Hoyt? What in the world were you thinking?"

To which I replied, "Fortunes were being made overnight, Mommy. I just hit a bad streak. For a while there I did wonderfully."

"Wonderfully," she said, with a sharp edge of sarcasm in her voice, but she came through for me. By this time, she had herself undertaken financial ventures, into the stock market, and had done marvelously for herself. She easily afforded the assistance she provided me.

The second venture which turned sour on me was after I again relocated, this time to upstate New York, the Troy-Albany-Schenectady region. This venture had to do with land itself, not what might be under it in the way of mineral deposits of any sort. This time I couldn't afford to go back to Wisconsin for her assistance, achieving this by long-distance telephone.

"I do *not* believe this, Hoyt!" she said on the phone from Milwaukee. "Tell me this is not happening again!"

I confess to being partially in my cups when I phoned her. The failure of this venture was especially devastating to my emotional makeup, which accounts for the drinking behavior I continue to cope with as best I can. "I think I'm snake-bit, Mommy! Somebody up there doesn't like me! Somebody up there's got it in for Hoytie Rademacher, whatever I do!"

She said, "Are you a burden I'll carry to my grave, Hoyt?" And she said, "Have you been drinking?" Of course I lied, said, no, I was stone-cold sober, just distraught. And she did agree to provide the assistance needed to get me out of the state of New York.

Financial ventures are gambles. So, I thought, why not cut through the wrapping, just cut to the core of it? This led me to Nevada, where I experienced alternating streaks of good and bad luck, both at casino tables and wagering on sporting events. As I suppose was inevitable, I encountered a bad stretch of sufficient duration to land me in debt to some very unsavory persons who demanded payment, making only thinly veiled threats to do me bodily harm. I did fly to Milwaukee to make this appeal for assistance, knowing my mother planned to retire to Florida at any moment.

She said, "You take the cake, Hoyt! All you can ever see is pie-in-the-sky, isn't it! And I tell you I am disinclined to participate in yet another in your string of follies!"

"Mommy," I told her, "these guys are not joking. Do you want to see your Hoytie with broken legs or worse?" I sort of semi-lost it when making this last appeal, because I was truly afraid for life and limb.

"Never, never, never," she said, "come to me this way again, Hoyt! I'm an old woman, I've worked hard to earn my security. After a wretched start with your hopeless father, I've built a life that's successful and satisfying, and I won't have it jeopardized because my only blood kin in this world is an impossible idiot! Mark my words, Hoyt!"

"I do," I said. And I meant it. I felt certain it would never happen to me again. One good thing, at least for several years, that came out of Nevada for me was Marlene, who worked in one of the casinos I frequented. We married, then relocated to San Francisco.

I truly *do* believe there is some kind of curse or evil spell on me. My San Francisco ventures, which had to do with commodity futures, went well for a time, several years, and then did not. I came to realize I had nothing of my mother's knack for investment, and also came to realize I was not suited for the married condition, which Marlene also realized.

Which brought me to Ft. Myers Beach, Florida, to her Seaside Vistas. Where else could I have gone? What else could I have done?

*   *   *

"Mommy," I said when it got through to me she *really* wasn't going to help me out—this sixth time my fortunes collapsed on me. "Don't you love me?"

"You're my son, Hoyt, so I suppose I must, but I do not like you, nor do I respect you."

"You're awfully hard on me, Mommy," is all I could think to say.

"You compel me to be firm," she said. And she said, "I worked very hard after we left your father to give you the best in my power. I sent you to the best private academy in the state of Wisconsin, and I sent you to an excellent college. And what did you make of those opportunities." It wasn't a question.

All I could say was, "Wayland wasn't a good fit for my personality makeup. Ripon was OK, but I just wasn't cut out to be scholarly."

"You don't appear to have been cut out to be much of anything I've been able to discern in you, Hoyt. And then you married three women any man would know better than to tie himself to."

"I loved them. At least when I married them," I said. And, "People change on you over time. How should I know my marriages wouldn't pan out?"

"Indeed," she said. "And your business affairs are the proof of the pudding, aren't they." Again it was not a question.

"I've experienced rotten luck," is all I said. She snorted, sighed. I said, "What it is, Mommy, is I have this strong feeling of confidence I can make a go of it if you'll give me just one more shot at it." She laughed at that.

"I wash my hands, Hoyt," she said. She stood up. "My God, Hoyt," she said, looking out her balcony patio doors at the Gulf stretching away forever. "I'm at a point here at the close of life when I can do more good for you, and for myself, by ending it here and now this instant. Go away, Hoyt," she said. "Stand on your own two feet! Be a man!"

"I don't have any place to go to," I said, and almost lost it again, calmed myself, tried to think rationally.

"It's nearly lunchtime, Hoyt," she said. "I have a few of my crowd coming any moment. I don't want you here when they come."

"Are you saying to me you're ashamed of me?" I asked.

"It's beyond shame. You're beyond pity. Look at you. Go now, Hoyt!"

"I could stand to eat something too," I said, and, "I know how to present myself to advantage to people, Mommy."

"I asked you to leave."

"Can I come back?"

She sighed again, turned to me. "I don't see there's anything we can profitably discuss, Hoyt."

"You're my mommy!" I said.

"Oh, stop that drivel and just go!" she said. So I did, and for my lunch I found a Krispie Kreme and lunched on doughnuts, which didn't do my digestion any favors.

It gave me time to think, drinking bitter coffee with the Krispie Kremes I ate for my lunch sitting in my rumbling stomach like rocks.

I thought: What's going to become of Hoytie Rademacher, aged fifty-plus, in deteriorating health due to bad diet, chain-smoking unfiltered Camels, semi-alcoholic? I thought about the street people back in San Francisco, dirty, ragged, panhandling, sleeping out of doors in all weathers, living out of shopping carts. That scared me badly, made me shiver and shudder there in the too-cold air conditioning of that Krispie Kreme shop.

I thought about my three former wives, two of them still hot—or at least warm—on my trail for what blood they could squeeze of the turnip called Hoytie Rademacher. That didn't scare me as much.

I thought about the father I hadn't seen or heard from in nearly fifty years. Was he alive? Would my mother possibly know where he was? Would he provide me assistance if I could find him? My best memory of him was his always saying to me, *How's my fine boy Hoytie today?* If he knew me now, would he still love his fine boy Hoytie?

But I knew she wouldn't know where he was after all those years, didn't care if he was dead or alive. When she set out on a new life, when I was aged seven, she totally cut loose from the old one. And why would my father care to help his fine boy Hoytie if I should by some chance show up with my hand out?

What it was, I thought, was that Hoytie Rademacher was all through. I might just as well be dead, except I wasn't yet.

Which, thinking about being dead but still alive, got me on to think-ing about my mother being aged seventy-six. If she were to pass away, I let myself think, who else but her Hoytie would she bequeath her assets to? What surprised me, trying to digest those heavy doughnuts, was I didn't feel much by way of guilty qualms for thinking that, and *that* did make me feel some true guilt.

But I also thought: Fat chance of my mother passing away in any near future! She looked healthy to me, strong as ever, not a quaver in her voice, no hesitation in her step, her life full of friends and cultural and recreational activities.

So suddenly I was feeling very, very sad, imagining my mother stand-ing at my grave site as they buried me, a modest service. Or would she perhaps decline even that, one more handout to Hoytie Rademacher she'd refuse to provide? That made me a little bit angry, her turning me down even in death, which in turn made me feel foolish, getting angry over what had not happened.

What I did was go back to her Seaside Vistas. Where else could I have gone?

"Hoyt," she said when I buzzed her apartment, before I could an-nounce myself.

"Did you have a nice luncheon with your crowd?" I asked.

"Hoyt," she said. Her voice was very hard, very firm, over the inter-com. "No, Hoyt," she said.

"Mommy," I said, "I need somewhere to stay! Only a little while. I don't have any funds for a motel or anything. Please, Mommy!"

She was silent for a little while that felt longer. Then she said, "I re-main resolute, Hoyt."

I of course naturally lost it again, there in the Seaside Vistas entrance-way, sweating hard, wheezing despite how cold the air conditioning was. I confess I blubbered. I said, "I think my life's over! And it's like I never actually had a *real* life! I think I want to go jump in the ocean and drown if you won't put me up! Just for tonight, Mommy! Please," I said between my blubbering, "it's your son Hoytie! You have to still love your son!"

And she buzzed me in, said, "You're making a scene!" And she put me up on her sofa, which had one of those beds that fold out from underneath, because her second bedroom she called her office, where she had her computer and file cabinets, a desk and an office chair on casters. She even gave me dinner, even a glass of wine with it. I could have used something stronger, but she said she drank only a glass of wine per day because it was good for the heart, for which she also took a daily pill. And I felt a little better; it sort of indicated my mother *did* still love me.

"Your heart's probably sounder than mine," I said.

"That's nothing I care to speculate about," she said to that.

She didn't set up the sofa bed for me, but got out sheets, a pillow, a light throw for a blanket. When she turned out the living room light to go back to her bedroom, I said, "Goodnight, Mommy. I love you very much."

She said, "Goodnight."

I said, "Are you *really* saying no to me, Mommy?"

"I am resolved," she said, and said, "I'll give you breakfast in the morning, Hoyt, and then you *must* leave."

And that's what I had to go to sleep on. I did a lot of thinking, but nothing came of that. All I knew was Hoytie Rademacher was on a slippery slope in the direction of the grave, and his mother had ample assets to relieve his situation, but would not. Her last will and testament was a possible solution, but her prospects were better than mine with respect to longevity. I listened to her running water in the bathroom, saw the light from her bedroom go off. Then there was just the dark, the thrumming of her air conditioning. I thought: this is what it feels like when you're dead and buried and nobody loves you, not even your mother.

I enjoyed a deep sleep. I don't recall dreaming, but suppose I must have. I have a lot of dreams, usually, when I sleep, mostly involving anxiety and varied threatening circumstances. But I'd like to think I dreamed pleasant dreams that night in my mother's apartment on her sofa bed. I'd like to think I dreamed of when I was a child with a father and mother who loved me as much as I loved them. It would be nice to have dreamed I was a fine boy with the best of potential personality and character inherited from his two loving parents, sure to grow up to be a man of charming personality and strong character.

I hope I dreamed positive dreams of my former spouses, of the times early on in those marriages when we were in love and thought our marriages were sure to last for life. I'd even like to have dreamed good dreams relating to my varied financial ventures, of my mostly unsavory and untrustworthy associates, of those periods when we were successful, certain we were on the brink of significant affluence.

I so wish I'd dreamed about myself as a youth and young man, with my mother's good looks and strong character and whatever good things were in my father showing up in me, personable and determined and energetic and disciplined against life's many problems to come.

But I don't recall dreaming. And then I was fully awake, surprised and confused for a moment as to my surroundings, morning light flooding the apartment, the glistening Gulf out the balcony patio doors. I popped off that sofa bed in my underwear, thinking about the toilet and hopefully a shower. Then I saw the clock in her small kitchen, saw how late it was. I was surprised I slept so long, wondered if my mother always slept so late in the morning.

I must have waited an hour at least, marking time there in her apartment, waiting on her to get up. I went out on her balcony to smoke Camels, watched packs of gulls way below, little white spots on the beach, watched flights of pelicans skim the water, looked out at the Gulf, some sailboats, the water stretching away forever. I prowled the apartment, trying to keep quiet. I checked out the fridge, orange juice I drank from the plastic bottle, checked out her second bedroom, her office, all the file cabinets, her desk and chair, computer. If my mother had a last will and testament—of course she did!—was it in those files, maybe in her computer? I didn't shower, didn't want to without her express permission.

I did some thinking. I thought about how cramped and sore I felt from sleeping on the sofa bed, about what I could possibly say to her to make her relent on her resolve to send me away empty-handed. I thought again about the homeless street people of San Francisco, getting up from wherever they slept the damp night outdoors, going off with all their belongings stuffed in a shopping cart, setting off to panhandle for another day. I didn't lose it, though I got a little teary-eyed, and my breathing got rough and wet, but I stayed pretty calm.

When I couldn't wait any longer, I went to my mother's bedroom door, stood there a while before I could make myself tap gently on it. There was no response. I tapped again, said, "Mommy? Are you awake?" When I got no response, I tapped a third time, and her door popped open a little. So I opened it all the way, stepped in. She was still in bed, turned away from me, lying at an unusual angle, sort of cross-wise on her bed. I said, "Mommy?" again, and stepped closer, then went around the foot of her bed.

Then I saw my mother's face. I don't know what I felt. Her eyes were half-open, but I could tell she wasn't seeing anything. I bent down to look closer. There was no motion, no breathing. I said, "Oh, Mommy!" I guess it came to me very slowly that she was gone. Gone in her sleep while I slept deeply without dreaming out on her sofa bed.

What I thought about then is mixed. I felt horror and shock, naturally enough, and hurt and sadness. I thought about what I had to do, what I should do. I felt a kind of thrill, because my mother's passing meant she would be saving me again, a sixth occasion. I felt great guilt for thinking this. I could not make myself touch her, so I picked up her little bedside phone and dialed 911, and it wasn't long before they came and took her away. What I remember wishing was that she had said something besides *Goodnight* to me when she went to bed the night before. I wished she had said she loved me still, even if she wouldn't help me anymore. Maybe that would have been what I truly needed, done the trick?

The last thing I remember thinking was that mix of thrill and guilt. And I thought about how I would have to go through her file cabinets, find her last testament, maybe try to get into her computer if that's where she kept it.

It was very strange after I was alone there in her Seaside Vistas apartment, which I guess I understood was probably mine now. First I'd cry, long and hard, because I'd lost my mother, had nobody now. Then I'd be very calm, considering all the details I'd have to attend to, organize myself. I remember I looked into her bathroom mirror after I had my shower, which I badly needed, and caught myself sort of smiling. Not truly a happy smile, but a sort of expression of contentment, well-being.

And it came down to two possibilities I have not as yet resolved:

Either my life was over, Hoytie Rademacher was done, finished—who knew the actual state of my mother's financial affairs? Who knew how she might have disposed of her assets in her last testament? Or else, and I confess how pleasing this feeling was, Hoytie Rademacher had just begun a whole new life, aged fifty-plus, yes, but a fresh start, like being born anew.

Though with no one left to love him, and wondering if anyone ever really did.

And What Should I Do in Illyria?

"And what should I do in Illyria?
My brother he is in Elysium."

—*Twelfth Night*

The last time I saw my brother Art, our reunion was unplanned, un-expected. My wife answered the phone, and I set my book aside on the chance it might be for me, a student or colleague with a last question or request; it was what we call Dead Week in academia, a vacationlike lull between the end of class meetings and final examinations. I marked my place in the book, prepared to get up from the recliner where I do my reading, grade papers, watch television, ready to go to the phone if Gloria called me.

Instead, she brought the receiver on its long cord to me, clasped against her chest. "Your brother," she said.

"Now what would prompt that out of the blue?" I said, getting up, holding my hand out for the phone.

"You're asking me?" she said, then gave me the phone, turned and left the room. I took a breath, put something like a smile on my face, turned away from the direction my wife took out of the room. I didn't suspect she'd try to listen, but I knew how much she disliked, disapproved of, Art, knew I would be uncomfortable speaking to him if I thought she overheard.

I exhaled, put the receiver to my ear, said, "Art. This is a shocker. To what do I owe the honor?"

My brother said, "Paulie," and, "Can you get single for the night?"

"What?"

"Are you free tonight?"

"Where are you calling from, Art?"

"Downtown," he said. "What passes for it in this burg of yours."

"Here?" I said. "You're in California now, right? Or have you switched base again?"

"I'm downtown," he said, and, "I'm passing through. I fly out in the morning. Come on down," he said. "I'll buy you dinner and drinks."

I said, "It might be nice to give a person a little warning in advance, you know?"

"Then it wouldn't be a surprise." My brother told me where he was staying—an old but still posh hotel downtown—to meet him in the bar in an hour, sooner if I could make it, hung up without saying good-bye, a telephone habit of his.

I walked the receiver back into the hall, saw Gloria standing at the sink just inside the kitchen. "Art's invited me to dinner," I said, and, quickly, "He's apparently just in town for the night. I doubt I'll be late."

My wife spoke without looking at me, said, "Spare me the details."

I said, "I won't go if it's going to bug you. I can call his hotel."

"Don't be childish," she said, still not looking at me. "He's your brother."

"That he is," I said. I dropped the buzzing receiver onto its cradle, stood for a moment, not sure there was any point in saying something more to Gloria. And I said, "I don't plan on being particularly late."

"I don't plan on waiting up for you with a rolling pin, for God's sakes."

"I guess I'll change into something," I said, and when she said nothing more, left her in the kitchen, went to the master bedroom to dress for downtown, the old but still posh hotel my brother Art stayed at. His finances, I thought, must be in an up cycle to pay the rates there.

I had not seen my brother for almost four years, not since he visited—unannounced—with his then third wife, Melissa, one in a string of occasions accounting for my wife's dislike—*detestation* is more accurate—of him.

It's a constant puzzle, a mystery to me. How can brothers, perfect parallels in blood and upbringing, be so dissimilar? I know better than to expect us to be as alike as, say, twins, but still, our common parentage, our shared childhood and youth, should, I think, have worked to mold us in some far more shared patterns of character, personality, and experience. We are—we were—almost polar opposites, as if one of us had been a foundling, unrelated.

From this earliest time in our lives, I sensed this profound, essential difference between us, and began to strive to erase it by the strategy of imitation. The younger by three years, my attempts to emulate him always fell short. I'd like to know the hours I wasted on playgrounds and ball fields, in gymnasiums, trying to become the athlete he seemed to be so effortlessly. How much of my sensibility was squandered in affecting his dress, his stance and walk, the glib speech with which he charmed our parents, his teachers, friends, girls? How scarred am I to this day by the anguish I felt, all the way through high school, at my failure to resemble him to even the slightest degree?

I remember one of his pals—he was very popular—a senior like Art, stopping me in the hall my freshman year in high school. "Hey," he said. "You're Art Nelson's little brots?" He towered over me in his letter-sweater, a look of mild irritation on his face.

"Yeah," I told him, "Paulie Nelson."

"I will be dipped in shit!" he said, and, "I'd never guessed you was related until this here one guy said. I knew he had a brots, but not you I didn't."

"Well," I said, "I'm his brother." He walked away from me, chuckling, the heel taps on his shoes clacking on the tiles.

Without the accidental junctures of history, I can imagine I might have spent the whole of my life this way, running after my brother, driven to catch him, slowed by the burden of that need.

Because Art waited a year after graduation to start college—he did not quite finish—I did the same, so was drafted, age nineteen, sent to Vietnam, which in the end I have decided was a kind of blessing. I have no war stories, no trauma; I served as what we called an R.E.M.F., out of harm's way as a supply clerk at Long Binh, but my tour was enough to break, or at least loosen, my oppressive link to my brother, and made all the difference in what my life has turned out to be. Art, in college after his year lying fallow, was of course deferred, then never called, drawing a wonderfully high number in the lottery when that time came.

I envied his luck then, but have come to feel maybe I was the lucky one, as things turned out.

The bar of this old but still posh hotel was in keeping with a decor popular in the forties and fifties, an atmosphere of overbearing dimness coming from the massive dark woodwork, muted lamps casting small circles on white tablecloths, large, indistinct paintings in heavy frames, no music, the long bar itself a kind of oasis of subtle light making brass fittings and the polished bartop flare in spots, the backbar a misty mirror fronted by rows of bottles topped with chrome spouts, the tall beer tap pulls collared with pale ceramic. The bartender, formal in white jacket and bow tie, parted his slicked hair in the middle, sported a mustache with waxed tips. He leaned forward on his hands, listening to my brother Art, perched on a tall, padded stool, one shiny shoe on the rail.

Art turned to me as I walked in from the upholstered lobby, spoke loud enough to embarrass me, though the room was nearly empty, the cocktail hour crowd not yet assembled. "Looky, looky," he all but shouted, "it is Mr. Paul himself, out on the prowl."

"Hello, Art," I said, put out my hand. He took it, squeezed hard, a salesman's grip, his other arm circling my neck, yanking me close for a bear hug. I smelled his cologne, hair oil, shaving talc. Released, I stepped back, breathed deep, as if I surfaced from under water, starved for air. "You're looking good," I started to say.

"Shep," Art interrupted, "this is my little bro, Professor Paul, the family brain. Does he not look the part to a T?" The bartender leaned across the bar, shook my hand. He wore a small badge on his white jacket, white plastic, the hotel's coat of arms, *Shepard* in slim black letters cut into it.

"Your brother speaks well of you," Shep said, waxed mustache tips wiggling like antennae.

"I hope," I said.

"A round! A round!" Art said, knocking the bartop with his knuckles. I tried to gauge my brother—how far along on the way to drunk was he? I didn't know when he must have dropped AA. He drained what looked like a martini on the rocks, nudged the thick glass at Shep, who raised his eyebrows at me, twitched his mustache—what was I having?

"I guess a draft," I said.

"Screw a draft," Art said, and, "Mix the man one of my concoctions there, Sheppie."

"Can do," Shep said, turned from us to work over his silver shaker.

"It's early in the day for me to hit the hard stuff," I said.

"What are we, punching a clock here?" my brother said, took out his cigarettes, offered me one. I shook my head no. "Balls," Art said, "you swear off? Surgeon General scare you, Paulie?" he said. Shep set our drinks before us, made a note on what must have been Art's tab, stood back, folded his arms, ready to talk or be invisible, a good bartender. We raised our glasses, Art clicked his against mine, said, "Bumps," and we drank. "First one today," he said, "or does memory deceive?" I laughed with him.

Though I could see, after four years, Art had aged, added weight to his waist and jaws, a touch more gray lacing his dark hair, my brother was still a very good-looking man, impressive.

His hair was still thick, cut longer than men his age did these days, his posture straight, teeth strong, white as china, revealed in the confident, open smile never absent from his lips. He had the kind of stature and structure allowing him to wear clothes with distinction. His red blazer with gold buttons, dull silver tie, slacks holding a knife-blade crease, glistening shoes, were all too sporty for this staid venue, but I felt we forgave him—Shep and I—if only for the sheer vitality he projected into this ostentatiously grim lounge.

"You *do* look like a prof, Paulie," he said, reached out, caught the corduroy lapel of my jacket with two fingers, rubbed it like a haberdasher testing for substance, quality. He wore a big watch, the sort one can wear sky-diving or scuba fishing, a very large stone in a plain setting on his pinkie. He had not worn a wedding band since his first divorce.

"It's what I am, Art," I said. My hair is lighter than Art's; I have a very small balding spot exactly on my crown, easily combed over when I take the trouble. I pay little attention to what I wear; my wife Gloria chides me for this. While I'm two inches shorter than my brother, I'm almost as lean, but somehow I wrinkle what I wear, everything feeling and looking a size large for me. I wear the kind of shoes one does not need to shine.

He drank faster than I did, rattled the ice in his glass at Shep for a refill. "So," he said, squaring himself on his stool as if he prepared to deliver a rehearsed recitation, "how's Gloria doing? Still sweetness and light?"

"She's fine," I said, and, "I think you two are constitutionally incapable of appreciating each other's qualities," allowing us both to laugh.

"The boys?" he said.

"Good," I said. "Artie's still in grad school, Cliff's getting somewhat serious with a gal I met only briefly, but she seems OK to me."

"He still in school, too?" I nodded yes. "It must be higher education in your damn genes, Paul."

"It could be worse, the way the world is today," I said.

"There's nothing wrong with the world," my brother said, and, "Now I'm supposing you wonder what brings me to your fair little town, right?"

"You want me to guess?"

"I doubt you could," Art said. "To be blunt," he said, "I'm on my way to an unlikely place called Marietta, Ohio."

"To do what? You leaving California after all these years?"

"Twofold," my brother said. "Uno," he said, tapping one forefinger with the other, "there resides there a woman by name of Lucille, of, as you'd probably think, somewhat tender years, who, I'm proud to announce, has agreed to join her fortunes with mine. Secundo," he said, extending his middle finger, "I am, however temporarily, betwixt engagements. In plain English, unemployed, and this young Lucille seems to think prospects are ripe in Marietta, Ohio, for a man of my many talents." My brother grinned at me, lifted his fresh drink without avert-ing his eyes, waiting for a reaction.

"Christ, Art," I said. "So what happened to what's her name, Peggy?" He laughed loud and hard.

"Ms. Peg and I is done broke it off, as they say, though you'll recall it was never sanctified by clergy." I never met Peggy, who followed Melissa, who followed Kay, who followed Marge, mother of Art's only child, my niece Patricia.

"You should put out a scorecard," I told my brother.

"Be sure and tell your beloved spouse," Art said. "I know how enter-taining she finds my life and loves."

"I will if she asks me."

"Drink up, you're lagging," he said, and I did, though I did not like the taste of gin, the burn in my throat and chest and stomach.

My brother did not like talking about the past. When I asked, he told me he had not spoken to Peg since he moved out of her condo, had no idea where his second and third wives were, had no real contact with his daughter beyond receiving Christmas cards—he sent her a birthday check when he had the money. "Margie's still married to the same dope she married after we went through the mill," he said, "which I know only because Patty writes me little notes on her Christmas cards."

"That's sad," I said.

"Everyone has their own life."

"Don't you ever try to imagine how things might be if they were dif-ferent?" I asked my brother.

"Sure. I just order two more of whatever I'm drinking," he said, raised his glass to summon Shep. "That cures it right quick."

Only because I insisted did we get something to eat. If I had not, I sus-pect we would have sat there until closing. Art said he was not at all hungry. "Fine," I said, "but I've got to eat something unless I want to float home, OK?"

"Party Poop Paulie," he said. When Shep brought us the tab, I reached for my wallet; Art grabbed my arm, tossed a credit card on the bar.

"That's pretty generous for a man's out of work," I said.

My brother said, "Instant money, just add ink," and signed for the bill.

"Your brother's quite the character," Shep said to me as we got off our stools.

"You could say that," I said. I was amazed Art could walk so well, no hint of stagger or sway in his gait as we left the hotel to find a restaurant. I had the feeling, though I looked only straight ahead as we walked out, that people turned to watch us, him, that it was as much an occasion for them as it was for me. I had the feeling there might be light applause, but of course there wasn't.

There is a picture, a studio portrait our mother arranged to have made when I was seven, Art ten. We are seated on a piano bench, a colorless, shadowless drapery hung behind us. Art has his arm protectively around my shoulders, my head resting against his chest, his free hand covering mine in my lap. This picture conveys a blatant image of the older brother's care and concern, his love for the younger, but my expression gives it away. Art smiles broadly, eyes lit with energy, his seated posture almost cocky. I am not quite scowling, my mouth shut in a pout, eyes listless; it is clear I do not like the pose, barely able to hold still for the photographer's shutter, that this pose is false. I do not remember the actual studio session, but our portrait says, I think, so much about me and my brother, the fundamental distinctions between us.

I was more than a bit unsteady on my feet, but willed myself not to show it as we walked only a few blocks. Art found us a good restaurant, one I would have considered beyond my pocketbook if I were taking Gloria to dinner. There was an elegant woman to greet and seat us, a clean-cut boy to pour our water, a dignified, mature career waiter to take our drink order, a very attractive woman to bring us menus, heavy as photo albums, gold-tasseled, the dignified man again to write our selections in a bound notebook, and, when the meals were served, a small corps of assistants to the dignified gentleman to carry them to our table in a procession, lay them before us.

"Very tony," I said to Art, hand shielding my mouth for fear I'd be overheard.

"Enjoy," he said, "it's on me," waggled his credit card at me.

"I can't let you do that, Art." I wondered if I had the means in my wallet to pay my share.

"Hey," he said, "how often do I get to see my baby bro?" and, "You never will learn to enjoy yourself, will you, Paulie."

I was not surprised we had to have two martinis before dinner, not surprised the food was mediocre—this restaurant placed its emphasis on service and appearance—not surprised Art did not eat much.

"So when'd you drop off the wagon?" I asked my brother.

"I didn't *drop*, I jumped!" he said, and, "If you knew the kind of people go for that stuff, you'd run for cover, too," he said, and, "Look at it this way, I'm not supposed to eat because of my blood pressure, I'm not allowed to drink, I'm as good as married, so no sex, right?"

"Very funny. I heard AA was all types."

He said, "They're like you, Paul, they're so fearful of screwing up their lives they don't dare live them."

"Drinking hasn't screwed yours up?" I said.

He said, "You don't hear me apologize for anything."

I am not accustomed to drinking so much, so perhaps it was gin that made me bold. I said to my brother, "You don't approve of me or my life, do you, Art."

Art said, "That's different. You're my favorite brother, in addition to which you're my only." And he laughed, but I didn't.

"Let's just enjoy the food at these prices."

"Now you're talking," my brother said, and laughed, and I laughed with him. "We'll get us a post-prandial and some coffee, then I'll see if we can't find a place that barkeep Shep was telling me about, supposed to be right around here."

"What place?" I asked.

"Says it's a blast," Art said. "Place with some action."

"It's getting on to my bedtime."

"You always were a party poop," he said, and, "Come on, see how the other half lives."

With my veteran's benefits, going to college made perfect sense. And I found I had learned enough discipline in the army to enjoy study and the contemplation of ideas for themselves, without necessary reference to the world around me. And I had seen enough of mixed humanity in barracks to want something that would keep me above and away from the absurdities and disasters and pure chaos that animated it.

While I made my way through four years, then grad school, Art went out into the world with great energy, directionless, but enthusiastic, and sometimes successful. I used to wonder at the bizarre ways he found to earn a living, that he seemed to almost prosper, would have prospered if he'd stayed long enough in one place.

I went through college, lived frugally on my educational benefits, lived with our parents, came very close to making Phi Beta Kappa, was convinced by several of my teachers I was suitable for their profession, made plans for graduate school. Art did a lot of different things.

The first job he had, still living at home, was selling Bibles door to door; I suppose he answered a newspaper ad. And he sold a lot of them. "Did you know, Mr. Smarts," he told me, "your average woman is good for three Bibles in her lifetime? *Three.* One when she gets confirmed, another when she gets married, a third when her kids start going to church. It's a statistic." He showed me his wares, Bibles ranging from plain to plush bindings and covers, gold and silver stamping options, bonus color renditions of the Sacred Heart, and his closer, a portrait of Jesus he called The Bearded Lady, the one with blue eyes and delicate feminine features, surrounded by pink-yellow light. "If I can bullshit them to this, they're mine, brother!"

When he lost his job, despite great sales, he said it was a personality conflict and an argument over commissions with his group supervisor, but I have come to suspect it was complaints from housewives who smelled liquor on his breath at mid-day, perhaps a sales manner so aggressive as to border on threatening?

He left home to go on the road with a character he met at a racetrack bar in Chicago—he had developed a semi-serious interest in gambling. "You'd love this guy," he said to me. "Must be sixty if he's a day, been doing this since who laid the Chink, works when he feels like it, man, has he got it knocked!"

This character—his name was Cy Burke—traveled the entire Midwest in a panel truck, small town to small town, offering his services to cemetery trustees, sandblasting gravestones, weathered for generations, clean as new. "I learn the ropes, Cy can't live forever, I go on my own," my brother said, "I'll make a damn mint!" I don't know if he could have or not, though he did it for most of a year before winter shut down the tour.

"You going back out in the spring?" I asked.

"I don't think so. There's better ways to turn a buck."

Then he gambled professionally. Chicago in the summers, Florida in winters. I think he made a decent living off the horses, made money playing high-stakes cribbage with other touts in bars, but gave that up after less than two years. "So you're not getting rich?" I said.

"I'm doing OK," he said, "but if you calculate the hours I spend on dope sheets, plus living in motels, restaurant meals, it's a treadmill."

"You should go back, finish your degree."

"I don't need a union ticket," he said, and, "I leave that to you, numb-nuts."

Then he went into business for himself, started a window washing company. "How do you start a company?" I asked him.

"Easy," he said. "You print up some business cards, you buy a bunch of buckets and rags and soap and some ladders and what-not, you hire a gang of kids to drop your cards all over hell's half-acre, hire some niggers to do the work for minimum wage, you're in business."

"Where do you get these inspirations from, Art?"

He tapped his temple with his fingertip, said, "Imagination. You have to have imagination. Vision," he said.

I don't think he made money at that, but then he began selling new and used cars for a Ford dealer, drove a demo, did well, but was fired, he admitted to me, for drinking on the job. Then my father used his insurance connections to get him on with a small agency selling automobile policies to high-risk clients, and there he made a lot of money, I think.

And there he met Marge, his first wife. Our parents didn't know she was pregnant when they married—my niece Patricia—and were very happy to see him marry, settle.

I was the best man. Just before we walked out to stand at the altar, I said, "I want you to know I sincerely do hope this is going to make you a long and happy life, Art."

He said, "Paulie, behind every good man stands a good woman . . .

with a hook in his ass!" He guffawed, and I laughed with him because it was his wedding day. I assume that, Marge unwilling to get an abortion, marriage was less complicated than running away, that he wasn't ready for that sort of solution yet.

The place Shep the bartender recommended was called Gents. I knew such places existed, of course, but could not have named one, would not have been able to find one on my own. Art said, "Now we're talking!"

There was a ten-dollar cover charge. Art paid for both of us, pulled what looked like a fat bankroll from his pocket, slipped a twenty from his silver clip, handed it over with a flourish. "Are you printing your own now?"

"I cashed out when I split from old Peg, sold my wheels, stereo, the works. Travel light, travel fast," he said.

The doorman, bouncer, whatever he was who took the twenty, said, "Table or bar, boys?" I looked for an open table in a corner, in the rear, somewhere I hoped we might talk in normal voices.

Art said, "Oh, bar to be sure! I gots to see this up close," and steered me, hand in the small of my back, toward a pair of empty stools.

"You accustomed to joints like this?" I asked my brother.

"Feast your eyes, Paulie." It was a long oval bar, lit by colored over-head bulbs that flickered to make a dizzying strobelike effect. There were poles like firemen slide down to their engines, set, bar to ceiling, every fifteen feet or so. And dancers.

These women were topless, wore g-strings and high-heel shoes, dancing to the music racket, one at each pole. Each gripped a pole, a sort of base from which to undulate, bump and grind, hunch and thrust in ap-proximate time to the music that hurt my ears. They were tall, leggy, big-breasted women, girls, their faces masked in makeup, skin flecked with glitter, mottled by the purple and gold and red lighting.

There was a kind of podium in the middle of the long oval of the bar, a kind of disc jockey who worked switches and levers to control the lights and music, a fat young man in a cowboy hat who seemed totally absorbed in his work. The bartender was also fat, wore a tank top, his shoulders and chest and arms blotched with tattoos—snakes, skulls, nude women.

"You got to be kidding," I leaned close to Art to speak through the music into his ear.

"The form divine!" he shouted back at me. He ordered drinks for us, slapped a fifty on the bar when they were served, took a dollar from his change—I could not really believe the price of a Gents drink—stretched up from his stool, reached out and tucked it beneath the g-string of the topless woman who writhed about the pole nearest us. She stuck her tongue out at him. "Do it for daddy!" he yelled at her.

I pulled him close to me, near screamed, "Arthur, I feel like an asshole in here!"

"Jesus, Paulie, go with the flow just once, will you?" He leered up at the woman. She leered back, but did not stick her tongue out again until he held up another dollar; she bent nearly double to take this one in her teeth.

I looked away, scanned the crowd, mostly men, but there were some couples. The people at the tables, lit only with tiny candles inside orange globes, did not watch the dancers. It was all men at the bar, almost all of them with heads tipped back, half-smiling, half-gaping up at the pole dancers. A few looked depressed, staring straight ahead at nothing, down into the drinks they nursed. My brother was the only one bantering with the dancers, as if he were our group leader, director of the show. I wondered how I looked to anyone who might turn my way.

"Art," I said to my brother, "I'm really not at all at ease here."

He said, "Drink up," and, to the woman who had his two dollars, "Grind those beans!" Art snapped his fingers, pumped his leg to the drumbeat. I resigned myself, wondered what Gloria found to do with the evening, tasted my drink—it tasted watered.

"Get nasty!" my brother barked at the dancer, who turned away from him, spread her legs, bent forward, mooned him, wiggling her behind only inches from his face. "Do it to it!" Art hollered, got a smattering of applause from some of the customers.

"Do they ever take an intermission?" I do not think my brother heard me.

I think women, as much as alcohol, were my brother's downfall. Whatever time in his life I think of, there were women. In high school, there were cheerleaders, a kind of chattering, giggling chorus flirting out-rageously with him, drawn to him for his exploits on the court and the ball field and gridiron. In college, there were sorority girls, vying to wear his ring or fraternity pin. He seldom boasted, took this unceasing atten-tion as his just due. While I dated some, I was not forward with girls, women.

I was best man at his wedding to Marge, the only one there besides the bride and groom who knew they would be parents in seven months. I was not surprised when they divorced when their daughter was three, surprised it lasted that long. He did not seem affected by this, moved back home for a short time. "You know you broke Mom's heart, don't you?"

"Hey, Paul, you make a mistake, you correct it, you move on, OK? I'm supposed to put up with crap because my mom's all bent out of shape over it?"

"Correct it," I said. "You pay child support for the next twenty years."

"I can afford it." And he could; he did very, very well selling auto in-surance to high-risk clients. One of them was Kay, his second wife. There was no wedding ceremony, just a sudden trip across state lines— Art thought Kay was pregnant.

She wasn't, and they divorced as soon as they were certain of this. Like Marge, Kay was a beautiful girl, glamorous, a fitting wife, I thought, for my brother. I liked her, was sorry when she moved away, disappeared. Art said to me, "The rabbit lived, so what's the point? I'll get over it."

He did seem to get over it, with Melissa. Art was tired, I think, of hearing about his drinking, tired of lost weekends and hangovers. He met Melissa at an AA meeting, and I was a witness for this wedding, held in a judge's chambers, along with Gloria, who I met in graduate school. A month later, they moved to California, to start over, Art said, build new, sober lives. "Maybe three's the magic number," I said.

"There's no magic about it," Art said. "I have nothing against boozing except it's expensive and it tears you up if you don't control it. I *can* drink if I want to, I just choose not to." I doubt that's what they taught at Alcoholics Anonymous, but it seemed to work for Art and Melissa, at least for a long time.

Art and Melissa moved to California and prospered—I gather almost everyone did in those days—sent me a very large check when Gloria and I married, just after I finished my doctorate, called and apologized for not coming home for the wedding. "I'm sorry you can't make it. I want you to know Gloria, she's an excellent person," I said.

He said, "If you say so, that's good enough for me." Gloria was offended he did not attend.

Art was never a letter writer, but we spoke every few months on the phone.

It was Christmas. "Merry Christmas, Art," I said, smiling at my wife and young sons, our decorated tree.

"To be sure," he said, and, "I need to give you my new temporary address."

"You moved?"

"I'm moving. Melissa and I are separating for a while here."

"You getting divorced again, Art?"

"Not if I can help it," he said, and, "They have a little thing out there called community property, right? The bitch isn't getting her mitts on my dough that easy."

"How do you do it?" I asked my brother. "How the hell do you live that way, Art?" My wife was frowning at me.

"Are you kidding? Man, I am raking it in hand over fist. You should think about coming out here, Paul, make a real living instead of pissing your life away professoring."

"I don't think so."

My brother's life made me all the more certain I had found the right path for mine. I was a good husband, a good father, good professor. I was sorry Gloria detested him, but she had heard too much from me to see him as anything other than our black sheep. I never considered him that; he was my brother.

"I can hardly believe you're related," she said.

"I feel the same sometimes," I told her.

"I'd go out of my mind married to someone like him."

"Well you're not," I told her. "You're married to me." She only met him a few times, the judge's chambers, the two trips home he made for our parents' funerals, once with Melissa.

"He treats me like I'm part of the furniture," Gloria said. "Does he have the vaguest interest in anything except himself?"

"Gloria," I said, "we buried our father. He's not likely to be disposed to be sociable."

"He says smart-aleck things," she said, "and I don't think he's got a scintilla of interest in Artie and Cliff. I smelled liquor on his breath," she said.

"It's just you and me now," I said when I put him on the plane to California after our mother's funeral.

"You're all right," he said. "You've got a whole family of your own."

"So do you."

He said, "If you mean Pattie, that's a damn joke. If you're talking about Melissa, that's an armed truce, not marriage."

"You think you'll last with her?"

My brother said, "Not one damn second longer than I need it to." It lasted several more years, until, I think, Art found some way to protect his assets against community property. I lived my life, raised my sons, taught my students, achieved the security of academic tenure.

When he was ready, Art divorced his third wife, went to live with Peggy, who he did not marry, wise, I presume, to the high price of California divorce law.

"How like him," Gloria said.

"Very," I said. At the time, I believed Art had a great deal of money, thrived in the coast's real estate boom. And somewhere thereafter, still with Peggy, he jumped, as he said, off the wagon.

It was nearly closing time at Gents, the crowd down to a morose few, the dancing over. Semi-drunk, I watched the disc jockey cowboy shutting down his console, putting tapes away, watched the fat, tattooed bartender run his closing register calculations, focused on the drink before me, tried to clear my head, shake the blur out of my vision. Art had talked one of the dancers down from the bar with his dollar bills, onto a stool beside him, sat knee-to-knee with her.

He pivoted to me, said, "I want you to meet my favorite brother Paul. Say hello to Kandy Kane, Paul," he said. Close up, out of the hard overhead lights, she looked both young and old, grotesque in her make-up; she had bad skin, a protruding belly, dirty ankles above her high-heel shoes.

"How do you do?" I managed to say, and, "I'm about on my way out of here home."

"The hell you say," my brother said. He said, "Now, Miss Kandy Kane, tell us your real name so we can get friendly."

Kandy Kane said, "Winifred." Art whooped.

He said, "Now tell me if there's a house specialty I might like to take you up on."

Winifred Kandy Kane said, "I do table dances and I do lap dances."

I said, "Art, I need to get out of here before I fall on my face."

My brother said, "Miss Winifred, I was thinking more when you clock out here, maybe we could arrange a sort of private party."

I said, "Art, don't."

Art said, "And could you perchance come up with a friend for my brother here? See, he don't get out of the house much, so this is an occasion." I meant to say something, but my tongue went numb.

Winifred Kandy Kane said, "There's this one friend I could maybe call if I'm getting you right."

I said, "No, Art. No."

He said to her, "Hold that thought a sec," patted her knee, kept one hand on hers on the bartop, turned and leaned close to speak into my ear. "We'll go back to my hotel, have us a party."

"No, Art," I said, and, "I'm getting up and leaving if I have to crawl out of here. I don't even remember where I parked, but I'm going home. Jesus, Art."

"Some brother you are," he said.

She said, "If this is on, I have to go call now or it might be too late."

"Paulie?" He sat back on his stool, looked at me, half-smiling. He did not look at all drunk. It was like a test.

I said, "You're forgetting Lucille in Ohio."

He said, "What Lucy don't know ain't no skin off her teeth. Gloria either," my brother said.

"No," I said. I said, "You think I lived this long to make a life to blow it off just because you zip in feeling randy? No, Art."

My brother stopped smiling, said to me, "You're a real barrel of laughs, Paul. You always were." I got off my stool, reached for my wallet, determined to put every cent I had on the bar. "My treat. Shove off," he said.

Winifred Kandy Kane said, "So should I ring my friend or not?"

"Enjoy yourself, Art," I said, and walked out of Gents, concentrating to keep from swaying or stumbling.

"Bank on it!" my brother called after me. I stopped at the door, looked; he was grinning at me, had his arm around Winifred Kandy Kane's bare shoulders. She looked confused. I tried to wave a good-bye to my brother, but think it must have looked as if I were waving him away, dismissing him, which is not at all what I meant.

That was the last time I saw my brother Art.

We had just started the new semester when the call came. Gloria answered the phone, called to me. "It's some person named Lucille Hickey," she said.

"Where's she calling from?"

"Marietta, Ohio?" Gloria said.

I said, "That's that." So I spoke, just that once, to Lucille Hickey, calling from Marietta, Ohio, to tell me of my brother's sudden death—a heart attack, an aneurysm, the local coroner thought. He died in his sleep, must have thrashed or groaned, but did not wake her. In the morning, when he did not move, respond to her voice, she touched him, found him cold.

And that is where he is buried, Marietta, Ohio, in a plot owned by Lucille Hickey's family. For several good reasons, I did not go to my brother's funeral. And I will never go to visit his grave.

I think: it is only natural to be sad. I have lost my parents, my only brother. It is only natural to be somewhat depressed.

I think: what very different people we would have been, how very different our lives might have been had Art and I been not such total opposites, been, somehow, the more logical combination of such different qualities of character we possessed. If Art had my stability, my direction, my focus . . . if I had some of my brother's energy, his confidence, his natural talents, some of the sheer force of his personality . . .

I think: for much of my life I tried to be what he was, for much of it measured myself by what he was not.

I think: put your brother behind you, turn to what *is,* a loving, loyal wife, fine, decent sons, a respectable profession, such credits to who and what you have been, what you are.

I think: Art was an alcoholic, a drunk who made and lost much money selling whatever came to hand, Bibles, auto insurance, real estate, God knows what else. Art was a lecher who marred the lives of at least four women—how many others?—fathered a daughter he abandoned without hesitation or remorse. Art was a lasting sorrow in the hearts of our parents. Art was an unmitigated failure, the black sheep my wife would call him if we were to speak of him.

I think: I am steady, reliable, a good man, husband, father, teacher. I am accomplished, if only in unspectacular ways.

When I chance to think of my brother Art, I catch myself feeling as if he were still alive, as if I still yearned to be something like him, as if I still took satisfaction in knowing I was nothing like him.

Elder's Revenge

"I wish," Elder's wife, Selena, said, "they'd never found your address."

Elder said, "Don't start. Please," he added, not wanting to sound harsh, not wanting anything to distract him, spoil it. He said, "You can still come with."

"No meant no, Harry," she said, and she said, "That'd put a fine crimp in your style, wouldn't it, show up with a person of color—do they say that in Oklahoma?"

"You know I'm proud of you," he said quickly, and, "You'd be the hottest attraction there, there's not a one of those hick broads could hold your coat. Do it," he said, "come with."

"Oh my dear man," Selena said softly, and stepped up close behind his chair where he sat at his desk, checking to see he had his ducks lined up ready to go. She put her hands—her lovely, delicate, long-fingered brown hands—on his shoulders, leaned down and kissed the top of his head lightly, smack on the barely perceptible balding spot he combed over and sprayed in place to conceal.

"You do know I really want you with?" Elder said.

"Yes," she said, and, "Yuckie. Your hairspray tastes metallic!"

"It's odorless, Dr. Elder," he said, turned to look at her, but she had already turned away, left his study without speaking again. "Onward," Elder said aloud to himself.

He had his ducks lined up. His plane ticket, first-class, the confirmation for his rental car at the Tulsa airport—the biggest, the most luxurious, Elder insisted.

He drove a Lexus, the twin of his wife's, forty-eight grand and change with the trimmings, had hoped Hertz or Avis or Exec could match it, but felt OK with the Lincoln Towncar, top of the line available. He'd considered a chauffeured stretch limo, but that was over the top. The trick, Elder understood, was just enough restraint to impress with equal parts of ostentation and a clear indication he wore his good fortune with ease, had taste, no need or desire to blow his horn.

Elder truly loved his wife, but was glad she would not attend with him. The rednecks in the class of '68, which he calculated at about 50 percent, possibly 60, would have seen nothing beyond Selena's color. He imagined: *You see Elder and his old lady? You remember Elder, right? Doofus? Jesus, he married him a nigger woman. I shit you not!* He shook his head, banished the generic voice.

He was ready. Money. Mostly fifties, not hundreds, but all new bills, crisp as fine bond. The plain brushed silver clip, no need to dig out his secretary wallet to flash. The Rolex, a subdued model, Selena's good taste last Valentine's. Pen and pencil, Cartier, though he figured the class of '68 wouldn't know them from Cross or Hallmark. Briefcase, all satin leather and polished brass fittings, solid as a block of oxblood granite, combination lock, its jaws open before him on his desk, a selection of documents, correspondence with the right letterheads, thin files, a calculator, cell phone, Danish import laptop computer no bigger than a placemat, hard warrants for anyone who dared doubt or question.

A laminated glamour studio portrait of Selena, another Valentine's gift, if anyone started showing pictures. She was exquisite, only a couple of shades darker than Lena Horne, a touch more Negroid in her features. He smiled, imagined a generic classmate, the student council or class officer type, showing family snapshots, bad candids of overweight wives and homely offspring in those cloudy little plastic windows sold in dime stores.

"Ho ho!" Elder mock-laughed aloud in his dim study. "Hee hee!" He snapped the briefcase's jaws shut, twirled the combination's tumblers, stood, went through all the first-floor rooms looking for Selena, hoping she'd join him in a nightcap, a ceremonial toast to impending triumph. But she was already tucked in upstairs when he got to the master bedroom. He made deliberate noise in his bathroom, so knew she only pretended sleep as he slipped in beside her, knew it best to pretend he did not know this.

He let himself lie deeply into the caressing sheet, the whole of him relaxed, confident, certain he would sleep deep until his alarm woke him with classical music. And he did sleep, but it was troubled with vague dreams of panic in crises, incoherent moments like film clips in which Elder faced impossible odds and Hobson's choices. He woke early, Selena really asleep beside him, lay abed, waiting for the music, killing time with the catalogue of his astounding successes in life, his brilliant future, the store on which he had fed since receiving the reunion invitation.

They did not speak in the breakfast nook, but just before she entered the elevator to descend to their underground garage, her Lexus, heading for her clinic, she kissed him on his chin, said, "Have a good time, Harry."

"God," he said, "how I savor the smell of you morning fresh!"

"Be good," she said.

"Oh, I will," he said, thought she was actually smiling at him as the elevator door glided shut, swallowing her. It *will* be good, he thought, was tempted to do his *hee hee* aloud, but felt foolish at the thought, so got his things, drove his Lexus to the airport in the silence of early morning. The last thing he checked in the vanity mirror before he turned it over to the parking valet was his hair, felt his confidence surge as he noted how well his comb-over obscured that damnable balding spot.

Elder's flight was unremarkable. He sat back in the wide, cushioned first-class seat—there were only two others in the cabin, seatmates, mid-level oil company management men from the little conversation he cared to eavesdrop. He drank a Bloody Mary, thinking he had to pace himself at the festivities, be a man accustomed to bending the elbow without evidencing any overweening pleasure or indulgence in strong spirits. He tried to doze, but couldn't, so had the cabin attendant fetch his briefcase, took the yearbook out of the false bottom's secret compartment, leafed, checked his memory one last time.

There they were, the class of 1968, and he knew them still, almost all of them. The rednecks, sons and daughters of blue-collars, oil patch labor, scratch farmers and scrub cattle ranchers, their faces broad and dull, wide-set eyes, boys' hair cut to the maximum length allowed by the dress code established to stifle the impulse toward any hippie or doper look, girls favoring the straightened long hair and bangs to imitate the likes of Cher and Grace Slick. The rednecks—fully 60 percent?—would be easy.

The boys would be, Elder was sure, gone to sprung guts and scarred hands, work-worn, driving pickups, weathered by the Oklahoma sun, dried hard as venison jerky in the low humidity. The girls would be bottom-spread with childbearing, coarsened with beer drinking and meat-and-starch diets, gaudy with nail polish, hair dyes, and thick, sweet perfumes.

Elder hit the lavatory, examined his hair, only a little longer twenty-five years later, his face no less lean, features improved by the chiseling of time, his body fashionably slender and tight from aerobics and the service of a personal trainer, hands smooth, his eight-hundred-dollar Arnold Constable suit—light gray, not at all somber—with vest a perfunctory signal of his affluence. His contact lenses were a world away from the metal frames he wore from the age of ten. His sprayed hair, cut at a cost of two hundred dollars in a salon patronized by two congressmen, was perfectly teased to fullness, nary a thread of white in it. He remembered his father's shaggy, unruly locks, his mother's fat bun, brown to the day she died, and thanked whatever powers for this blessing of genes.

Back in his seat, he declined the attendant's offer to serve him a second drink. "I have some driving to do when I hit the ground," he said.

"Reunion?" the steward said.

"How'd you guess that?" he asked, alarmed.

"Your annual there. College? O.U. or Aggie?"

"High school. Ponca City," Elder said, and, "Very perceptive on your part," and they both laughed. He leafed his yearbook.

The cliques. The cliques would probably not be so easy. They had the head start, sons and daughters of money, influence—*clout* was the word Selena, who grew up on Chicago's Gold Coast, used. They'd have clout still, the ones who played safe, stayed on in town after an obligatory degree down in Norman, took over the insurance agencies, real estate brokerages, law firms, followed the trail through O.U. Medical to doctor and dentist Ponca City's middle class, some ascending to refinery management with Conoco. And those, like Elder, the few who left at once, it was possible they'd made it even bigger, stockbroking and financial consulting, high tech engineering, a C.E.O. or two. But just as possible they failed in the big world. Elder crossed the fingers on both hands, wished a wish.

And the girls in the cliques, the true lookers with style and a thin finish of grace, they'd have made the effort, kept weight off, bought their clothes in Tulsa and Oklahoma City, Dallas fashions, and always the chance some married winners, rose beyond the local country club and community arts council, had no more than two children, sent them to private school, to out-of-state universities, came back for the reunion for the sheer mean pleasure of walking like absentee monarchs taking a tour through a province conquered long ago, come back to say—Elder imagined it, a brittle, well-modulated voice, Okie twang refined out of it: *Do you see? I stood above you then, unreachable, untouchable, see me now I stand yet higher, so far above, beyond you. I think you see!*

He could not stop himself finding her page. Charlene Eldridge. German class. Geometry. Geography. Always beside, in front of, just behind Elder, fate driven by the alphabet. And him. Bart C. Jones III, Mr. Ponca Everything. He squirmed in his comfortable seat. Slapped the yearbook shut.

Elder summoned the attendant, had a second Bloody Mary in hand before he could continue his leafing. He found them, found himself, the nerds, doofuses, creeps, outcast lepers of the era 1964–1968, the homely and ungainly, awkward, athletically inept, socially ignorant, emotionally inward, stunted and stunned. There he was. Oh Jesus. *Harrison V. Elder,* his pathetic activity credits: *Service Club. Cineasts. Boys' State. Volleyball. Esperanto Club.* Harry the Brain. Jesus! Elder thought, felt himself shrivel in his first-class seat, felt the sour, electric emptiness blossom just below his sternum, the blighted flower of his adolescence blooming after a quarter-century dormant to poison him again. Jesus.

Then he remembered Death. There would have to be a necrology in the program they passed out. How many dead of accident, Vietnam, hereditary malfunction of hearts and kidneys and livers and thyroids? Cancer. This did not cheer him—there was no coping, no argument, no victory over the dead, fled from the field before battle joined.

He locked the yearbook away in its secret place, could not finish his drink, closed his eyes, resisted the desire to groan like a man on the brink of profound nausea from having eaten too much too fast of some confection once loved, long abstained from.

The drive from Tulsa International to Ponca City revived him. The Lincoln was pristine with new-car smell, rode like a big yacht on smooth seas, air conditioning an unobtrusive hum, steering excruciatingly sensitive to his touch—no Lexus, but the essence was there. He found some classical on the stereo, the N.P.R. station at the A & M in Stillwater—the ambitious among the rednecks of '68 would have gone to be Aggies. And he found strength and new resolve in the desolate landscape of north-central Oklahoma.

This also was what he had escaped from, won over. Low rolling hills dotted only with spindly stands of blackjack oak, thin lines of willows tracing the courses of shallow streams already shrinking to trickles in the early dry season that set in after the spring thunderstorms, any of which could explode into tornadoes. It was desolate pastures beginning to tinge brown, feeding scrawny cattle, and Elder felt himself swell with pride—it didn't get him!

He had money. Lots of money, work of genuine importance—Harry Elder consulted with the Pentagon and NASA, work he performed with joy, performed outstandingly. He had a half-million-dollar home and a place on the Jersey shore, and he had Selena, beautiful and brilliant and so exotic she might have come from another planet than the one he zipped across in his rented Lincoln Towncar. And he was coming back home, one last time, to let everyone know he, Harrison V. Elder, was risen in fortune to happiness. His rented Lincoln was no Lexus, but it would do. He sailed past Keystone Lake, striped bass capital of the world, whipped by the Stillwater exit ramp, cut north toward Ponca City like a shark changing direction to seize its helpless prey.

He looked up from the road to smile a big smile in the rearview mirror, comb-over solidly in place. He deliberately thought of them. Charlene Eldridge. Bart C. Jones III. Their graduation portraits in the yearbook, their haunting, taunting faces through those high school years a vicious collage. "Hee, hee, hee," Elder laughed his stylized laugh, his voice seeming to linger like a memorable music in the wonderfully cooled air.

But this spell collapsed, evaporated as he hit the outskirts. He had freed himself, totally, irrevocably, from it all, yet here it was, as always. It was the shacks where the ragged remnants of the Otoe-Missouria and Ponca tribes lived out their degradation on federal welfare, and the first view of Conoco's refinery towers and storage tanks looming on the horizon, and then the acrid stink of gas cracking, petrochemical acids, fouled the air sucked into the Lincoln to be chilled. It was ratty beer joints and quick-stops, the same white-trash housing, junked autos in bare-dirt yards, ragged wash on drooping lines hanging lank in breathless heat. An obese woman waddled to check her rural mailbox, a pair of burr-head boys, shoeless, shirtless, rode their bikes on the gravel shoulder, a man on his front steps, elbows on knees, chin in his hands, made an image so hopelessly forlorn, so doomed, that Elder hit the accelerator to leave him behind, reached the four-lane boulevard that would carry him to a better part of town.

He was relieved until he passed the statue of Pioneer Woman, unveiled and dedicated by Will Rogers in the twenties, saw to his mounting horror that the boy cowering in his mother's flowing skirts reminded him of himself, his mother. He broke the speed limit getting to the Marland Mansion, venue of the twenty-fifth reunion of Ponca City High's class of 1968, and the mansion's sandstone bulk calmed, soothed him as he pulled in the circular drive to the old coach entrance, stopped in its near-black shade.

Bill Marland, Elder thought, local, state legend, once thought he had won. Marland Oil came out of nothing, the wildcatter days in the Okie oil patch, and Bill Marland built this monstrosity he had no choice but to deed over to the city when his empire fell in on him in the thirties.

Bill Marland lost, but Elder had not, would not, and there was poetry in his sleeping in one of the suites where legendary Bill Marland, long dead, nearly forgotten, hosted the long dead, forgotten rich, famous, beautiful, and celebrated of his bygone day. Hee.

He sat only a minute or two in the Lincoln's air conditioning, idling, until a parking valet came out of the enormous wrought-iron and glass doors, got Elder's bags from the trunk, drove away somewhere behind a row of ornamental windbreak trees. A second boy came out to take his bags. They were teenagers, wore ill-fitting red jackets, nametags Elder didn't bother to read except for *Welcome '68!* He slipped the boy a twenty he found among the fresh fifties in his clip, said, "Split that with your partner in crime, we'll do it again when I'm on my way away again, OK?" He wanted *everyone* to know!

The boy held the bill's corner with the tip of two fingers, looked at it like it was foreign currency, then grinned, barked, "Yessir!" Elder had to motion toward the doors to get him moving inside with the bags.

He was grateful for the empty lobby, worried he might look even only a little travel-worn from his flight and the drive from Tulsa. There was only a desk clerk, another kid—*Welcome 68!*—to check him in under the banner hung from the vaulted ceiling. *Welcome '68!* It looked out of place in the ostentatious hall where Bill Marland surely welcomed his elite guests to balls and banquets and political and business confabs, playing lord of the manor while it lasted. The kid handed him the fat reunion packet, said, "You're on the early side, Mr. Elder."

Elder said, "Firstest with the mostest," and, "I'll take my bags up myself if you'll point me to an elevator." The elevator was large, played generic organ music as it rose smoothly to the penthouse, top of the line, premium priced. He entered his suite with a plastic card that clicked the lock open, and it was all he'd hoped for when he reserved it, all veined marble, wainscoting and flocked fabric wallpaper, smoky mirrors, gleaming bathroom fixtures, a jacuzzi and bidet, thick carpet, big-screen television behind inlaid sliding cabinet doors, king-size bed, fridge stocked with liquor, beer, soda, imported spring water, creamy stationery in the heavy drawers he opened to lay away his shirts and underwear and socks, a walk-in closet almost as big as his at home—

Hee! Elder thought. Wouldn't Bill Marland spin in his grave to see what became of his mansion!

He was early because he wanted time to ready himself, doff his travel garb, shower, primp and preen, redo his comb-over, dress for the first scheduled activity. But first he sat at the writing desk, opened the reunion packet, pad and pen to one side for notes on strategy and tactics.

The nametag—*Be sure to wear your nametag to all functions!*—was all wrong. It bore a reproduction of his yearbook portrait, so was most definitely out! Elder tossed it in the leather wastebasket. Let them ask who he was, who he had been. And he trashed a sheaf of flyers, local ads for restaurants, auto rental agencies, a list of merchant sponsors, Chamber of Commerce stuff featuring Pioneer Woman and Marland Mansion and Conoco.

He read the bios first, thin self-puffery and lame humor. He skimmed, found her. *Charlene Eldridge Jones. O.U.* One child, Melissa Marie. Another queen in the making? *Matron*—euphemism for *housewife?* Lifelong Ponca resident.

Too brief. No Junior League charity committee work? Country club? No hobbies or special interests? No statement on the quirks of Fate, the ultimate meaning of life as viewed from the vantage of a quarter-century? Was something wrong? Elder prayed it was so!

And where was Bart III? There, on the list of *No Response From:.* Something *was* wrong! A cold joy squirted in Elder's stomach, bubbled up his gullet, rinsed his mouth like a mint. Double-hee! Estrangement. Legal separation. Ugly divorce! Sometimes, he thought, staring at the pointless pattern of the wall's flocked fabric, it turns out better than your wildest dream!

And there he was: *Harrison V. Elder. M.I.T. Consulting Aerospace Engineer. The Pentagon. NASA. General Dynamics. Martin-Marietta. Married Selena Coleman, M.D. (Psychiatry). Enjoys foreign travel, symphonic music, contemporary literature, French cooking. Resident the past decade in Washington, D.C. (suburbs). Summer home on Jersey Shore.* Just enough, not too much, Elder thought, glad he'd labored as he did over what, how to say it when he filled out the questionnaire with Selena's help until she threw up her hands, told him he was making a quasi-psychotic mountain out of a neurotic molehill, laboring mightily to bring forth, at best, a mouse he wouldn't like when he saw it. He made a mental note not to forget to take the cell phone with him wherever he went—Selena had not promised to call, but might, and he prayed it came where everyone could see, eavesdrop.

Thank whatever powers, Elder thought, they didn't reprint graduation portraits with the bios.

He turned to the schedule. Attitude Adjustment and lunch poolside. The afternoon free, tennis, swimming, shuffleboard, circulate and reminisce. More Attitude Adjustment in the Marland Grand Parlor, then the banquet in the Great Hall. Announcements and remarks by class officers—who'd fill in for Class President Bart III? Recognitions. Prizes for farthest traveled to attend, most children. Booby prizes for fattest, least hair, most gray—Elder chortled. Champagne brunch and farewell the next morning.

He needed no notes, no plan of attack. He closed his eyes, breathed deep, exhaled loudly, opened his eyes, closed the packet, rose and set to his preparations for his appearance at poolside. He had recognized no names in the necrology.

Elder ran a last check in the mural-size mirror, too ornately framed, on the wall just inside the patio doors leading to the pool. Perfect. His white jacket set off the dark blue shirt, neck open an extra button to expose the thin gold chain—Selena's exquisite taste and boundless generosity—lying in the fringe of his still-dark, adequately abundant chest hair, collar tabs splayed outside the jacket for flair. Robin's-egg slacks, knife-blade creased, shoes shining like they'd been dipped in molten glass. He slid the jacket sleeves up just enough to feature his Rolex, fished his lightly tinted sunglasses from his breast pocket, donned them just as another of the kids in red jacket stepped up to open the patio doors for his entrance.

He stood in place a second on the green concrete to adjust to the burning Okie sun in the vacant near-white sky, then moved toward the small crowd in and around the cabana shading the bar. Nobody in the pool, the surface tilted back and forth, little ripples throwing off reflected sunlight like steel shards. *Now,* Elder thought.

He felt let down. Only a few men and women turned to watch him pass, one craning his neck to read the nametag that wasn't there, turned back with his drink to the woman he chatted up on the cabana's lip of shade. It was a little like being invisible, and he pointedly did not pause to read nametags, much less speak, moved steadily under the cabana, to the bar. "Vodka tonic, lemon twist," he said to the bartender, red-jacketed kid, who looked quizzically at him. "Stoly if you have it in stock, whatever's top shelf if you don't" Elder added, raising his voice to get above the small-talk babble surrounding him.

The kid said, "You're with the reunion party?"

"Class of '68," Elder said.

The kid said, "They's all wear a nametag."

Elder said, "I misplaced mine. Do you want some ID?" He showed the kid the edges of his teeth, sure he wouldn't mistake it for a smile.

"Nossir," the kid said. He had Stoly in stock, mixed, served him his drink. Elder folded a fiver into the tip cup. Then he stood, plastic glass in hand, and waited, surveyed the assembled covertly, looking for her, him. Not there. He knew an instant of panic. But then a tubby man, belly straining his buttoned jacket, garish tie, faded blond hair shot with dirty silver, put his face in Elder's, shared his astonishingly bad breath.

The tubby man said, "Harry Elder?" *Richard "Dickie" Mueller* read his tag, the face in the yearbook portrait striking Elder's memory like a sudden shaft of light cutting the dark. Dickie Mueller. Semi-doofus, too jolly all those years to deflect attention to his weight problem. But enough family money—Mueller Ford—to lord it over Elder, move with the cliques, at least on the fringes.

Elder said, "Hello, Dickie. You look prosperous. Selling lots of new Fords?"

Dickie Mueller guffawed, spoke too loud for that close to Elder's face. "You don't need a nameplate, Harry, I'd recognize you anywhere. How the hell are you?" he said, and, "I don't sell automobiles, I sell oilfield equipment, drilling mud, you name it. I sold my pa's dealership a dozen years back after he left us. Jesus, Harry, you haven't aged one iota!"

Elder said, "I haven't changed?" controlling his voice to mask a momentarily deep, despairing disappointment.

"Harry Elder the math whiz, Jesus, remember how we used to snap towels on your ass after gym? Maggie!" Dickie Mueller turned to shout to the dumpy woman just behind him, cut off Elder's protest that he did not remember towels snapped on his ass after gym before he uttered it. "Maggie, Jesus, here's Harry Elder, his old man owned the old hardware where Otasco is now, you remember, you had to be in some classes with him, right?" Elder had no time to clarify that his father managed the hardware, did not own it.

He read the dumpy woman's nametag: *Margie Laughlin Mueller*. Dumpy-fat Margie Laughlin, unchanged except for more fat, eyeglasses, a pronounced squint accentuating her crowsfeet, sickly-sweet perfume as she came close to take Elder's hand in her pudgy fingers, too-many-too-big rings on too many fingers, sweat beads on her fuzzy upper lip. She said, "I bet you don't remember me from Geography, Harry, I sat way in the back behind you."

"I remember," Elder said, bracing to endure them as long as he could. O.U. Married within a year of graduation, the campus chapel in Norman, five children, three at O.U. together right now. "No," Elder told them, "no children. I married late. My wife directs a psychiatric clinic in D.C., so she couldn't get away from patients to come with me."

"You seem to have done very well, Harry," dumpy Maggie Laughlin Mueller said.

"I suppose I have," Elder said, braced himself to expand on that.

But Dickie Mueller said, "Harry Elder the math whiz! You ain't changed a iota from the last time I laid eyes on you, Harry!"

"I'd prefer to think otherwise, Dickie," Elder said, but they seemed not to hear, talked over him about O.U., five children, the boom-bust cycles of the oil patch, and, no, they never considered settling anywhere else, Dickie's daddy's business and all.

"I vowed to strike out the second I graduated Ponca High," Elder got in. "I had a scholarship to M.I.T. maybe you recall. They announced it at graduation. Massachusetts," he said when they looked blankly at him.

"Sure, right," is all Dickie said.

"I read in the booklet they printed up," dumpy Maggie said.

And then they were gone, to the bar for refills, back into the growing crowd to circulate—*reminisce*. And Elder was alone, untouched drink in hand, scanning for Charlene Eldridge Jones, feeling near invisible again. No sign of her. He felt like weeping.

Thanks to whatever powers, this did not last.

He experienced a semi-epiphany, made sudden eye contact, mutual recognition with W. D. Norwood. W. D. charged up to him, big hand extended, squeezed Elder's like it was a strength contest, said, "Harry Elder! By God, boy, you look *good!* The years been kind to you, son!"

"You look pretty good yourself, Dub," Elder lied, delighted. *W. D. "Dub" Norwood* his nametag read, the yearbook portrait showing a thick, long shock of hair falling in waves where now W. D.'s bald dome shone in the sun like it was greased. And though he was still pretty trim, W. D. had grown a round pot belly that would have made a woman look six months pregnant. Elder grinned, tried to match W. D.'s grip, failed.

But W. D. Norwood, Ponca's star jock, asked Elder nothing of himself, his life the past quarter-century. He talked of the state senate, where he now held the safe seat his uncle occupied throughout their childhood and youth, retired only five years ago after a disabling stroke. Of course he was a Republican! Family tradition and good Okie politics in this district. Had a good to very good law practice—O.U. Law of course!—on the side. "Mostly worker's comp stuff, Harry, you make a lot of contacts in political life, and everybody wins with workman's comp," W. D. said.

"Who'd you marry?" Elder asked, hoping for reciprocity, but all W. D. said was Elder wouldn't know her, a girl from Yukon he met at law school, his partner now, she was somewhere in the crowd circulating, he'd introduce Elder if he could catch up with her, she was a pure pistol, and yeah, three kids, all girls.

"It takes a real man to shoot the balls off them is what I always say, Harry," W. D. said.

"I've heard too much testosterone is the cause of hair loss," Elder said, willing to say anything to make his point, but all W. D. Norwood did was cackle, run his palm over his shiny scalp, say that ran in the family too.

"What do you remember when you think back on it? High school," Elder said.

"It was a blast, every minute of it was a ball!" W. D. said, and said he'd go fetch his wife to meet Elder if he could find her, left after another painful handshake. Elder took a gulp of his vodka tonic, clenched his jaws so tight he half expected to hear his molars crack. He remembered

Dub Norwood playing varsity football, basketball, baseball, punching Elder's shoulder—hard!—whenever he stood in line near him, calling him Pencil Neck, four-eyes for the wire-rim specs Elder wore until he got contacts after graduating M.I.T. At least W. D. Norwood was cue-ball bald with a six-months-gone pot belly!

And then Cecil Turner sidled up to him, introduced himself. Cecil Turner hadn't changed beyond usual aging—gray, gaunt, scars on his sunken cheeks where rampant acne, air-brushed out of his yearbook picture, raged from puberty onward. Cecil Turner was no good to talk to—he was a fellow nerd, geek, in charge of projection equipment, wore a ring of clattering keys on his belt to open all off-limits storage and supply rooms. He was now a teller at Ponca's BancFirst branch. "I'm actually head teller since two years, Harry," Cecil Turner said, and, "I guess you really made good, huh?" Exactly what Elder needed to hear, but not from a Cecil Turner. Elder was tempted to ask him, when Cecil said he was a bachelor, if he was the faggot everyone called him in high school, but could not, seeing the naked awe and wonder in his eyes. "I guess you surprised everybody, huh, Harry?" Cecil said.

Elder said, "It's no surprise to me, Cecil," and, "Do you remember Charlene Eldridge, Cecil?" Cecil said who could forget Charlene the Queen? "Jones now," Elder said. They married, no big surprise there, Cecil said, and not such a big surprise they divorced, asked why he asked. "Just curious," Elder said.

Then Cecil Turner said, "Well, so long, Harry. I got to go. I won't see you at the dinner dance and all. I'm not much on dancing and drinking and all. Congratulations on how good you did and all, Harry, I read in the brochure they wrote up."

"Thanks," Elder said, and took Cecil Turner's fish-clammy hand in his, wiped his palm and fingertips on his slacks when he stood alone again. Elder felt tears trying to brim in his eyes, was about to leave when a pair of plain women confronted him. *Carol Olson Fitz. Kimberly Karl Ray.* Elder had no memory of them.

"I took solid geometry and trig both with you, Harry," said the former Carol Olson. "You used to let me copy your problems."

"I went to Girls State the same year you went to Boys," the former

Kimmie Karl said. "We rode all of us on a bus." Elder asked them to forgive him, it was so very long ago.

"And you married a doctor!" Carol Fitz said.

"Psychiatrist," Elder said.

"I bet you're careful what you say around the house," said Kimberly Ray.

"No," Elder said, "I'm not." He felt blessed when they said, almost in unison, they were going to get their husbands, bring them back to the bar, introduce Elder.

The instant they were out of sight in the noisy crush, Elder fled. He had no appetite for the brunch they were starting to serve, and it was suddenly like the sock-hop pep rallies held Friday afternoons in the Ponca gym, everyone dancing, flirting, except Elder and the other handful of losers like Cecil Turner, standing off to the side, watching, hormones afire, isolated, alienated, ignored, as good as invisible.

There, in his penthouse suite—priciest digs available—Elder brooded through the long afternoon. All the veined marble, wainscoting, and flocked wall fabric like prison bars, the blazing Oklahoma sun blocked out by the heavy draperies, CNN on with the sound muted, he stewed in the juices of his simmering despair. It was no good, a total bust.

He couldn't recognize most of the gang of overweight, overdressed, over-happy nobodies clamoring for free drinks and brunch, and the few he spoke to satisfied not the smallest portion of his burning need. What the hell *did* he need? Confirmation, some certification in their collective, vacant eyes that Harrison V. Elder beat the long odds, ascended beyond anyone's craziest expectations—his own included—for him? Some stamp of approval of the man he had become from such humble, unpromising origin? Their admiration, envy? No.

Elder wanted payback, to exact an undefined retribution for the miserable adolescence he attributed to them—Ponca's class of '68! And he wasn't getting it, didn't see any chance of it in what remained of the reunion.

He almost threw in the towel, came close to calling Selena on his cell phone, confessing what a waste, what a futile gesture of self-serving this trip home was. Selena would understand, comfort him, forgive him the mean impulse that brought him halfway across the country to this long, sour afternoon holed up just like the social leper he'd been back then. But he stopped just short of dialing her at the clinic. His failure was more than he could yet confess—maybe later, back in D.C. as they shared a half-bottle of good wine from their cellar to celebrate his return. He wondered how much he'd lie when he came to the telling.

What he *ought* to do was rouse himself from self-pity, go out, drive the Lincoln to the Wanderer's Rest Cemetery, visit his parents' graves, place a wreath or flowers. He gave this up when he realized he was not sad for the loss of his parents; they were too much a part of what he had escaped, transcended. That they were gone to early, ordinary deaths seemed necessary, appropriate to finalizing his liberation from the pain of who and what he had been.

So, afternoon bleeding into early evening, Elder rose, bathed, dressed in his best, set his comb-over in place with unscented hairspray, girded himself for the scheduled extended Attitude Adjustment, the banquet and dance. There was always the possibility *she* would show. Something had gone nicely wrong—praise whatever powers!—in the supposedly storybook marriage of Charlene Eldridge and Bart C. Jones III, but that didn't mean one or both wouldn't show for the reunion's big event. And Elder wanted to be there, ready, just in case. To what end he wasn't at all sure.

Riding down in the soundless, liquid-smooth elevator, he was wholly confident. His jacket was pale green with a vague baronial crest on the left breast, his shirt even paler green with white collar and cuffs, his tie muted silver perfectly knotted, slacks snowy white, shoes white buffed suede. No draft, not even a stiff breeze, could so much as stir his coiffure, much less ruffle it.

But this deserted him as he stepped out into the lobby, followed the noise leading him to the bar in the Marland Grand Parlor, *Welcome '68* banner, bunting in the school colors. There was live music, some subdued rock, but the meld of gab and laughter, shrieks and shouts, overpowered it, and his first look at the assembled stopped him in his tracks, trembling. There were too many, too loud, all dressed as if for a solemn church service, though many boogied awkwardly, ineptly to the rags of the small band's nostalgia music. Elder saw them as a kind of monster, multiheaded, frenetic, a conglomeration of spasms, absolutely self-absorbed, self-contained, oblivious.

There was W. D. Norwood and a hatchet-faced woman doubtless his law partner–wife, the pair politicking a circle of classmates-now-constituents. And there were the former Carol Olson and Kimberly Karl, hanging respectively on the arms of their nondescript Fitz-Ray spouses. And Dickie Mueller and his fatty Maggie, bellowing and hyena-laughing. And there were others, faces he recalled as dimly as if he'd seen them only in nightmares, nameless, indifferent and hostile, and so he turned to go, return to his penthouse suite, pack, flee into the back east dark to Selena. And that's when Elder saw her on a barstool, looking as alone as he felt.

A quarter-century had touched Charlene Eldridge Jones with a less than gentle hand. She'd added pounds, not so much as to totally obscure the marvelous lines of her glorious girlhood, but there, a kind of gross padding attesting to the gradual, inexorable effect of Time. Her hair was dyed, her natural honey-blonde surely gone gray, now a chemical gold that flashed like brass in the harsh backbar lighting. But it *was* her! Elder made his way to her side, walking as easily as if he had the power to levitate but chose the ground ordinary folk trod, suddenly feeling invulnerable, shielded by some space-age force field sealing the two of them away from the raucous revelers cavorting all around.

Elder said, "Hello, Charlene," wondered at the depth and timbre of his voice, so long ago a half-squeak when excited. He said, "Is it possible you don't know who I am?"

She straightened up a little on her stool, frowned as she searched his face, her memory. Ah, Time left shallow tracks at the corners of her depthless blue eyes, now a little watery, at the corners of her full lips now painted too-red, had gouged an incipient double chin above the long throat now tending toward ringed and ropy. Charlene Eldridge Jones, Charlene the Queen, said, "You got a nametag or is this twenty questions time?" And Charlene the Queen drained her glass, sucked at the ice in the base, set it down hard on the reflecting bartop, looked back at him. There was a time, then, Elder thought, when such a look from her might have paralyzed him. He took a full breath of her syrupy perfume—remembered the delicate, clean coconut scent she exuded once—thought: *No more.*

"Let me," he said, caught the bartender's eye, summoned him with a wink. This kid wore a red vest, black sleeve garters, was trying to grow a goatee. "Two," Elder said, "of whatever," indicated her empty glass. He was surprised it was a vodka double. "Stoly," he said, "or whatever's top shelf here."

"Hoity-toity," is what Charlene Jones said, said it again when Elder found a ten in his clip, stuffed it in the oversize brandy snifter set out for tips. She raised her glass, he clinked his against it, was very surprised at how much of it she downed in a first drink. She said, "So how many questions do I get or will you just tell me your name and cut out the crapola?" While he tried to think what to say, shaken by her diction, she took cigarettes from her purse, gave him the time he needed. He lit a match from the book embossed with the Marland Mansion logo, held it out to her, felt what must have been his blood racing as she placed her hand on his wrist to steady it.

If nothing else, he told himself, he had experienced the touch of Charlene Eldridge's skin on his. It felt warmer than he had fantasized for years, a bit moist, though not quite sticky. Elder said, "I'm not surprised you don't know me. Elder," he said, "Harry Elder. Geography. English? Miss Loy's Latin class?" Her eyes widened—had she worn so much makeup around her eyes back then?

She said, "I sure as hell did not! Harry Elder," she said, and, "A Harry Elder stands here after a coon's age. Harry," she said, "I wouldn't have recognized you for that skinny little twerp always sat near me because we were both E in the alphabet, not in a zillion goddamn years. Harry the brain. You turned out pretty spiffy, you really wash up pretty good, Harry," she said. "You win the lottery or get a makeover or something, Harry?"

Elder paused a beat before speaking. It was *exactly* what he had traveled nearly 1,500 miles to hear, *exactly* what it had all been for. And yet not quite enough—what more was possible? He took a sip of his drink, noted how fast she drank hers, swallowed, said, "There wasn't any luck or chance involved, Charlene. I did it all by my lonesome."

"Tell me, I'm all ears," she said. So it was that they sat at the bar, self-absorbed, oblivious to all about them, and talked through the scheduled Attitude Adjustment of Ponca City High's class of '68.

What he wanted was to *tell* her, all of it, step by step, M.I.T., his spectacular professional success, the big money and the big house and the Jersey summer retreat, Selena, the sensational present and the boundless prospects of a future that obliterated the past they shared, but he knew it was necessary to focus on her. It was as important—more important?—to know what happened to her as to tick off the catalogues of his unimaginable good fortune.

He said, "So where's the ex-hubby? Bart the Third. Someone told me you two split up." She laughed, more a snort than a laugh.

"My gut guess would be getting sloshed to the gills at the country club unless they've cut off his tab again for nonpayment. Or chasing tail. Either way I could give two shits less," she said. And she told him the sordid, trite story of her marriage to Bart C. Jones III, infidelity and booze on both sides, financial worries that worsened when Bart's daddy left him a lot less than expected, legal separation and divorce with rancor over child custody—she had only a daughter, also a Charlene, herself married and divorced from a redneck Aggie from Hennessey, lived in Tulsa with a doper boyfriend. Elder had more than he could have prayed for.

"I'd like to say I'm sorry for Bart," Elder said, "but it sounds like he made his bed for himself. I'm sorry for you having to suffer it," he said, hoped he believed that.

"The sonofabitch," Charlene said, and, "He owes me back alimony and child support up the ying-yang, I could cut off his balls if I choose. And I probably will sooner or later," she said. When she asked about his marriage, he showed her Selena's picture, and she said, "Is she like Cuban or something?" Elder started to tell her about Selena's clinic, but saw her attention waver, eyes wander to the crowd pressing nearer.

"So what do *you* do with yourself, Charlene?" he asked. Nothing for a long time, but now sold real estate, did OK at it, belonged to a fitness club to work at her weight, but it didn't do the job. "You look good to me still," Elder said, did believe that.

"I'm a fucking mess," she said, and Elder realized how very drunk she was.

"That stuff has a lot of calories," he said when the red-vested kid served another round of double Stoly. Elder found another tenner for the brandy snifter, saw she noticed this, hoped it truly impressed.

"Like I give two shits," she said. She did not sway on her stool, didn't slur her words, but she was very drunk. There was nothing, Elder understood, he could not say to her, drunk as she was. He leaned his head close to hers, put a hand on hers as he spoke.

"Can you remember us in those classes together, Charlene?" Elder said. "I mean, *really* remember the way I do? You probably can't, because it didn't mean anything to you then. You didn't know I was alive, did you. You didn't know how it was like I worshipped you like you were some goddess, because you were perfect the way I saw you. You don't remember me at all from then, do you." He was very surprised by what she said.

She said, "I remember just fine. Alcohol hasn't affected my brain yet, Harry," she said, and now there was a slight blur in her speech. "You were a screwy little twerp always sat by me. Which isn't to say you weren't the school brain. You think I was a total zero didn't know what was going on with you inside your head behind those glasses you wore? I used to get a chuckle watching you watch me, Harry Elder," she said. She grinned at him, shook her head like she wanted to dislodge the memory.

When he could speak, Elder said, "Did it matter to you at all? That I felt that about you? So I was a twerp geek with thick glasses, four-point average, my daddy managed the shitty hardware store and dropped dead early from it, and my mom died because he died, but the thing I had was I thought you were God's gift, and I need to know did it matter at all to you then? Charlene?"

She shook her head again, blinked, and he held her hand tightly for fear she'd fall off her stool. She looked at him, smiled, said, "Can't say it did, Harry. Maybe I thought it was sort of cute or sweet, but I don't think so."

Now the crowd began to move, the music stopped, chimes summoning them to the Marland Great Hall banquet tables. "You ready to get some dinner and listen to speeches that are supposed to be humorous and nostalgic but aren't?" he said.

She looked at him for a long moment, blinked, said, "I think I'll be sick, Harry." She said, "I always drink too much and get sick, it happens all the time, but I always do it again the next time the same way."

Elder said, "I hate it that I didn't matter. I wanted it to have mattered." He said, "I could hate you for remembering I didn't matter. I never hated anyone so much except for myself, what I was then." But she didn't seem to hear him. She tried to dismount her stool, faltered, and he took both her arms, helped her, said, "We'll get some air, it'll be cooler outside by now," and he walked her out through the lobby, into the full dark that was much cooler now with a good northwest breeze.

"Where are we going?" she said.

"Let me show you my Lincoln," Elder said. "I drive a Lexus with all the trimmings. My wife, Selena, has one just like it. The Lincoln's a nice set of wheels though. You remember I never had a car in high school? Bart, now he had a car. You all had your own cars in high school." And he walked her around the Marland Mansion until he found the parking area, found his rented Towncar, leaned her against it while he fumbled for, found his keys, unlocked, and she half-collapsed on the cool, slick leather of the spacious back seat, and Elder slipped in beside her.

He didn't like the idea of what he was doing, but she seemed to expect it, helped him as he groped at her buttons, straps, elastic. He said, "It mattered. I mattered."

She giggled as he knelt over her, stymied by his belt buckle, said, "Little old Harry Elder. School brain. This isn't very comfortable," she said, "but it's not like it's exactly my cherry."

He got his buckle open, said, "You should have known. You should have cared. You clique-types," he said, "there was more to me than any of you, I showed you all," and then he said, "Jesus," because he had squirmed his trousers down, but was not ready, able. His thoughts cantered through his work, his money and stocks and annuity, the Pentagon and NASA, Selena, himself sitting beside or behind or next to Charlene the Queen Eldridge in classes, his insignificant mother and father in their graves. She reached up and ruffled his hair like she meant to snatch a hank for a souvenir. He said, "I don't think I can just right now."

She laughed, a loud laugh, said, "Big surprise. Little old twerpy nerdy Harry Elder. Better check that out with your doctor wife, Harry," she said, and said, "I'm sick I think." She pushed herself up on her elbows, leather squealing, shoved him aside, climbed out of the Lincoln, stood next to the open door and wretched loud and long onto the parking surface. She laughed, choked, vomited, feet set apart, hands on her hips, panty hose and pants bunched at her knees.

Elder, soul burning with shame and rage, writhed, zipped up, buckled his belt, fell back on the plush upholstery. Charlene Eldridge Jones cleared her throat, spat, said as if talking to herself, "Harry Elder? What in the fuck is wrong with me!"

Just as Elder was getting control of his breathing, his thoughts, his cell phone rang in his jacket pocket, but he was not frightened. He could lie to Selena by simple omission—that part was easy, though he couldn't muster his stylized laugh about that. And he could go back inside to the reunion, pretend nothing had happened, talk with any classmates who remembered him. He could tell them how well he had done in life, but he wouldn't tell them Selena was black.

What he wasn't sure of was if he could construct a lie big enough for himself, good enough, for after that, for the rest of his life, something he could at least pretend to truly believe in.

Learst's Last Stand

Let us swear an oath, and keep it with an equal mind, / In the hollow Lotos-land to live and lie reclined / On the hills like Gods together, careless of mankind.

—Tennyson

When Learst, on the run from Oklahoma, hit the outskirts of Tucson, he wanted to press on, push toward California or Mexico, wherever, but knew he needed a breather, a pause to get his bearings, focus on why he'd cut and run this time, lay out a more exact course for this third bug-out since Nam.

His Nissan pickup, all his worldly jam-packed in the bed under the camper top, ran like it was immortal, all the dash dials glowing steady and true, the ride smooth as the freeway concrete his tires licked like a ticking clock. And he didn't think he was fatigued, no more than a twitch of muscle between his shoulder blades threatening to pulse into a cramp. His eyes weren't burning after a full day squinting into desert sunlight like needles, his fingers didn't clutch clawlike on the wheel, no lead gathering in his feet, legs freed by the cruise control to shift and stretch at will. He had a near full pack of filter Camels in his shirt pocket, half a thermos of tepid coffee on the seat beside him, two Bud long-neckers left in the carton on the other side of the transmission's hump.

And now, under the cooling, dimming desert evening sky, after breathing air-conditioning for sixteen hours, he had his windows open, the air dry-washing him. He yanked out the cassette, let his ears rest. Learst felt *good,* up to another hundred—hell, two hundred miles! The digital said ten, central time, only nine here under stars clearer and thicker than over Oklahoma behind him, so why not keep going?

But the lights of Tucson came up slow ahead, like a reverse dawn in the west, and Learst had no tangible destination except away, so he decided, feeling the hard swell of his full wallet against his butt, to take the first motel showing vacancy—he'd get to sleeping in the Nissan before his disability check caught up with him. It wouldn't be the first time.

When the freeway became a four-lane road with a speed limit to match, he passed a neon strip mall, a couple of trailer parks, the fancy entrance to what looked in the dark like a country club or golf course or hospital, and then the street was a boulevard with palm trees and decorative shrubs, and then there were sidewalks, and then he spotted Desert Inn, slowed, *Vacant* in smaller neon, so he pulled in, shut the engine off, set the brake, got out, locked up.

He stood for a moment beside his truck, took in the black night, the stars softened now by streetlights and pastel neon, took a deep whiff of the warm, dry, odorless air, suddenly felt his body, stiff arms and legs, the hollow of hunger at his center. It was good he stopped; he was sore, weary, needed to rest and regroup.

The office was more small parlor than office. There was an unmanned counter, a color TV on, sound off, a sofa, a big recliner, coffee table with magazines, and three geezers sitting there, talking like Learst wasn't there with them.

"Yong Dong Po," one of the geezers said. He wore a sleeveless T-shirt, his arms and chest covered with blurred tattoos right up to his neck. "You know Yong Dong Po?" this geezer said to the other two. Without waiting for either to answer, he said, "Yong Dong Po, I run into what you're talking about, woman could suck the chrome off a trailer hitch!"

"You learned it," one of the other two geezers said. These two wore aloha shirts and walking shorts, tennis shoes without socks. One of them had a big turquoise and silver ring, and a big wristwatch set in a turquoise-silver bracelet.

"You don't need going to no Yong Dong Po," this third geezer said, "I got me some in Phoenix City first pass I had from Benning." The three geezers laughed, still like Learst was invisible, so he spoke up.

"Get me a room?" he said.

"Oops!" the first geezer, T-shirt, said, and jumped up like Learst's words goosed him, the other two standing like they were all connected.

"Get on the job there, Silas," the turquoise-silver geezer said. All three of them smiled at Learst.

"In a jif," Silas the T-shirt geezer said, and led Learst to the counter, gave him a registration card, pointed to a ballpoint pen chained to the counter. Learst registered, got a heavy key attached to a plastic tab with his room number and *Desert Inn* cut into it.

"I'm supposing it's too late for dinner here?" Learst said. "No?" he said when none of them answered. "Can you possibly recommend close by where I can get a good meal and maybe a brew or two?" They all three smiled at him.

"Coffee shop's closed after eight, you'll want The Blue Note," the third geezer said.

"Tell him The Blue Note, Silas, hell yes," the turquoise-silver geezer said.

"Blue Note's very popular with the fast set, two blocks up is all, you can't miss. It's a lounge," Silas said, "but they can whip you up anything from a cold sandwich to surf'n'turf with trimmings," he said.

Learst said thanks, and they all three smiled at him, took their seats at the coffee table again. Learst opened the door, turned back to them, said, "I know where Benning is, but where's this Yong Dong Po you said?" They all three laughed at that.

"Ask Silas, maybe he can give you her name," the third geezer said, and they all laughed at that.

"If she's as old as Silas she's likely dead years already!" the turquoise-silver geezer said, which caused another big laugh.

"Yong Dong Po," Silas said, "last time I saw it, is a scabby-assed farmer village about twenty, twenty-five clicks north out of Pusan," he said, "which is a port city of the Republic of Korea."

"Oh," Learst said. They looked at him, smiling. "Korea," Learst said. He said, "I thought for a second it could be Nam from the name, but it didn't sound like Nam not quite, the name."

"Vietnam," Silas said. "Merle here did a tour in Vietnam."

"Early on. '61," Merle, who was the third geezer, said. He looked just as old as the other two.

"I'm gathering you must of did one there yourself, did you not, young fellow?" the turquoise-silver geezer said.

"I did. I was just curious," Learst said.

"Nope," Merle said, "Yong Dong Po's a good name, not a dink one."

"It sounds it, now I think of it," Learst said. Silas and Merle and the turquoise-silver geezer smiled at him like he was going to say more, but Learst went out to find The Blue Note, two blocks up the boulevard, without speaking.

Coming out of the quiet night, Learst expected light and noise when he pushed open the padded doors of The Blue Note, was surprised, stopped in his tracks just inside by the dim interior, the only light a bluish sort of aura coming out of recesses in the walls. Everything was a soft, dim blue, the long bar, mirrored backbar with ranks of bottles on blue-lit glass shelves, tables ranging away to an even dimmer blue haze that had to lead to kitchen and lavatories. It was like coming out of bright sunlight into dark, having to adjust his eyes.

There was music from somewhere, the kind of dreamy stuff played on late-night FM stations, and beneath this the bubble of voices like another music. It wasn't crowded, but couples sat at more than half the small tables covered with cloths that looked blue-white in the lighting. A good half the barstools were occupied, couples again, pairs sitting facing each other, knee to knee, heads close like they were trading secrets. The Blue Note smelled like air freshener, the air nicely colder than outside. It was more cocktail lounge than restaurant, Learst thought, a sort of modified swinger's bar, upscale.

The bartender, stark white hair, trimmed black beard, red vest with silver buttons, black garters on his white, frilly sleeves, caught his eye, waved him over.

"Step right up, step right up," this bartender said, smiling a big smile that showed big white teeth, laying a napkin on the bar for Learst, setting a clean crystal ashtray next to it. Learst felt the deep carpet pile through his shoes, slid into a swiveling captain's chair three stools down from a couple who were all but mugging it up as if they were alone in the world. "I go by Skippy," the bartender said, putting out his hand.

"Learst," Learst said, took his hand. Skippy the bartender gave him a harder-than-normal squeeze, like he was selling insurance or used cars. Skippy the bartender's white hair was swirled into shape like pie meringue, a very black Van Dyke so thin it looked drawn on, black eyebrows under all that white meringue hair—Learst couldn't tell if he was younger or older than he looked. "They told me," Learst said, "down at the motel there I could get dinner here if your kitchen's open."

"No problema," Skippy said. He had a brushed metal nametag on his red vest, *Skippy P.* in black enamel. He said, "That would be Silas and his cronies. The Desert Inn?" he said.

"I think," Learst said. Skippy laughed, slapped the bar. He wore a big stone, fake or possibly real diamond, on his pinky.

"Good old Silas," Skippy said, and, "Did they hit you with the war stories?"

"I think I interrupted talking about Korea or something," Learst said. "I gather they're retired lifers? One of them said he was in Nam."

"That would be Otis I'd wager," Skippy said. "They're OK guys if you keep them off war stories, which is about all they know to gab about. So, menu?" he said.

"Please," Learst said.

"Coming up," Skippy said, and said, "Pre-prandial libation?"

"What?"

"Drink?" he said.

Learst considered. His impulse was maybe a beer or two with his dinner. He half-swiveled in his captain's chair stool, scoped the room. It was all couples, dressed up, all head-to-head-knee-to-knee like the couple three stools down from him, talking, nuzzling, a lot of hand-holding across tables, some sitting close enough to almost be in each other's laps, the women almost all bleach-blondes, the men with a lot of hair, elegant jackets, loud ties, the wink of gold and silver and fake or real diamonds on fingers, wrists, ears, lots of cigarettes. Learst could smell a hint of perfumes and colognes under the cigarette smoke swirling bluish in the chilled air before it was swept away in the ventilation. Yuppies? Learst wondered.

He'd figured a beer or two, but a drink felt more like in this Blue Note. "Vodka rocks," he told Skippy, who grinned and slapped the bar.

"After my own heart," he said. "Basics is best. Any preference? Absolut? Stoly?"

"Bottom shelf, house brand's fine," Learst said.

"Loud and clear," Skippy said, smiling, poured the drink with flourish, set it on the napkin, whipped out a butane lighter for Learst's Camel when he fished one out of his pocket, then went to fetch a menu.

It was while Learst ate his steak and potatoes and green beans that he noticed, had opportunities to swivel his stool, look close at The Blue Note crowd. This wasn't any upscale Yuppie hangout, no young swinger's bar. Everyone was old, years older than Learst.

Skippy, serving his dinner, pouring him a refill on the vodka, had to be in his sixties at least, judging by the papery skin of his tanned face, the raised veins and scattered liver spots on his tanned hands. The couple mugging it up three stools down were easily as old. The woman was in pretty good shape, but he could see her callused elbows, her ropy neck, crowsfeet at each of her black-rimmed eyes, heard her raggedy bronchial cough each time she drew on a fresh long cigarette Skippy leaned across the bar to light for her with his slim gold butane lighter with a big flame. And the guy she mugged with—that big head of hair all in place so near was obviously a rug. Learst couldn't make out the netting at his hairline in the blue lighting.

Everyone was old. The waitress running trays of drinks to the tables wore fishnet stockings, a low-cut blouse, but he could see her bony legs under the stockings, waffled upper thighs, her wrinkled cleavage when she passed close. The couples at the tables were all old, women with humps at the base of their necks, men with sagging chins and jowls and Milwaukee goiters pushing out their shirt-fronts when they got up to use the lavatories, rising stiff and slow, their walk the gait of old people who put one foot carefully in front of the other to hold balance.

Everyone was very old, The Blue Note like an old people's home throwing a party, a prom for old geezers dressed up to look young, hair dyed and bleached, heavy makeup, scents, acting like men and women one, maybe two generations younger out on the town, on the make, cruising. Learst felt suddenly strange, like he'd sneaked in where he wasn't permitted, like he'd plopped down in a foreign country where he didn't know any customs, couldn't speak the language.

Skippy cleared his dishes off the bar, wiped it, said, "A post-prandial?"

"What's that?"

"Drink," Skippy said. "Brandy? Drambouie? Or would you prefer to stay with the potato juice?"

Learst's impulse was to go, pay up and walk back to his Desert Inn bed, sleep deep and long, head out in the Nissan to wherever tomorrow. But he felt restored by the drinks, pleasantly full of steak and vegetables. This Blue Note was weird, the old crowd dressed and acting like kids, but he felt good even if he was out of place. He hadn't gotten blitzed since the long night in a cowboy bar in Stillwater, Oklahoma, when he decided to cut and run once more. Why not? Learst thought.

"Same old same old," he said.

"Dance with the one what brung you, right?" Skippy said, flashed his big white capped-teeth smile, scooped fresh ice into a new glass, poured with flourish.

"Join me in one," Learst said, took bills from his wallet, laid them on the bar. "Ain't no pockets in shrouds," he said, nudging the money toward Skippy.

"You can cut that one in granite!" Skippy said, poured himself a shot of something amber, saluted Learst, tossed it off like a kid showing off his drinking in some kids' bar like the ones Learst knew from Michigan, Colorado, then Oklahoma—all behind him forever.

So Learst hunkered down in his captain's chair stool, got blitzed on vodka rocks. Skippy kept his drinks coming, poured him at least two—Learst couldn't remember exactly—on the house. And Learst put them away, smoking Camel filters Skippy lit with his butane lighter. He was a good bartender, right there with the Smirnoff bottle when his glass emptied, always scooped fresh ice, a clean glass, replaced the dirty ashtray with a clean one, a fresh paper napkin when Learst's got soggy.

He blitzed himself, a classic shit-faced drunk, watched all the old geezers flirt and nuzzle, a few couples who slow-danced to the dreamy music coming from somewhere hidden, clutching like they wanted inside each other's clothes. He drank until the vodka lost its burn in his chest and stomach, went down cold and clean, easing him like sleep without dreams, watched the geezers move out in hand-holding pairs, talked to Skippy as business slowed toward closing time.

"You're a damn good barkeep," Learst said to him.

"I thank you, sir," Skippy said, and, "I should be, right? I was head barman in a five-star for years before I came to the promised land."

"Where exactly was that?"

"Nashville," Skippy said. "Just outside Nashville proper actually."

"You like it there? I never been in Nashville. All over hell's half-acre, but not Nashville."

"Nashville? A blast. Made in the shade. I was coining money, full medical benefits, pension plan, didn't exactly have to bust my cookies at it once you get your routine down."

"So why'd you move here?" Learst said.

"Mandatory retirement age," Skippy said.

"You're retirement age? You don't look it."

Skippy laughed, showed his teeth, whipped the Smirnoff bottle off the backbar. "I made a pact with the devil," he said, and, "That rates you one on me," topped off Learst's half-finished drink.

"I'm also retired somewhat," Learst said.

"Don't expect me to believe *you're* retirement age!"

"No," Learst said. "What it is, I have disability."

"Service?" Learst nodded.

"Ninety percent," he said. "I have to get recertified periodically, which is basically no sweat," he said. "I can live good enough on it without working," he said.

"You look fit to me," Skippy said.

"It's psychological," Learst said. He looked at Skippy, waited to see if the bartender would ask for particulars, but Skippy only nodded, smiled, moved off to do something or other down the bar.

Learst drank his drink on the house, had one more, bought Skippy a shot of whatever he drank, was finishing his next drink when he felt the room move, his stool swivel, his vision suddenly skew to near-double. "I got to split before I pass out on your bartop," he said to Skippy, who laughed.

"You are the last dog," Skippy said. Learst looked around, gripping the arms of his chair-stool against toppling over onto the floor. The Blue Note was empty. He hadn't seen the last of the geezer pairs leave.

"Jesus," Learst said. He let himself down out of the stool, one hand on the bar in case it swiveled and sent him sprawling. He set his feet, tested himself for sway. He was OK, could probably make it, he thought.

"Your change," Skippy said. Learst told him to toss it into the oversize snifter that held tips. "Appreciate it," the bartender said. "Take her slow, you're less than two city blocks from home, right?" he said.

"I'm thinking I can manage," Learst said, took it very slow toward the exit, sliding his shoes over the carpet like a skater, careful not to lose contact.

"Take care if I don't see you again," Skippy said. Learst reached the padded doors, braced himself with both hands on it before he half-turned to speak.

"Tell me, Skippy," he said, "how's come everyone's so damn old?" Skippy just looked at him for a moment before answering.

He said, "You're only as old as you feel they say, right? See anyone here tonight struck you as really *old?*" Learst shook his head.

"I may probably see you," he said, and, "Could be I'll hang around a while until I figure where in hell's half-acre I'm going." And he pushed out the doors, into the dark, before Skippy could speak again.

He was blitzed enough he had no true sense of the distance to his motel, no sense of how long it took him to stagger to the office, where he went in because he couldn't remember if he'd taken his key with him, couldn't remember his room number, couldn't make out where his Nissan was in the parking lot.

There were only two of the geezers sitting in the office now. The turquoise geezer was gone. "Ho ho!" the tattooed geezer, the one who registered him, said, "Somebody had *fun* at The Blue Note this night!"

"I know the syndrome," the other geezer said—what was his name?—said. "Two makes you feel good, it stands to reason four makes you feel twice as good. And so on. Am I correct?"

"Where's Otis?" Learst said, swaying, shocked he remembered the name of the turquoise geezer.

"Crapped out on us," Silas—he remembered the tattoos was Silas—said. There were empty beer cans on the coffee table, the television still on without sound. Did they tell their war stories all night? Learst wondered, leaning into the door frame.

"Went to hit the sack in his trailer if he knows what's good for him," Merle said—this geezer, Learst remembered, was Merle.

"Which you better do," Silas said. "Can you navigate or should one of us escort?"

"Just give me my key and point me," Learst said, not at all sure he could make it. Silas helped him find his key in his pocket, pointed him toward his room from the doorway. "I'll suffer for this come morning," Learst said as he shoved off.

"You dance, you pay the fiddler," he heard Merle say from inside.

"Not to worry," Silas called after him from the doorway. "Get up, hair of the dog bit you, bake it out in the sun. That's how The Blue Note gang does it, am I right, Merle?" Learst tacked through the parking lot, heard the office door close.

"Everyone's goddamn old as dirt!" he shouted up at the black sky. Concentrating, he got his room open, locked the door behind him, pissed like a racehorse, hoping he didn't splash the floor, let himself collapse onto his bed. As he passed out—he knew he was passing out, which was what he'd been looking toward from the minute he decided to get blitzed on vodka—he thought to himself he was glad he at least wasn't so damn old yet. Then he passed out, dropped into that pit where no dreams came, nothing.

By the time Learst woke, his hangover monumental, a classic to match the worst he could remember, it was nearly noon, the sun cutting between the slats of his room's blinds, hot light covering him like a blanket. His eyes popped open, this light hit him, and then he felt his iron headache, the log in his stomach, dead weight of his arms and legs and hands, his throat and mouth and tongue caked hard, the clothes he'd slept in pasted to his clammy skin. "Oh Christ," he heard himself croak.

He rolled off the bed, giddy, lurched to the window, peeked, squinting, out from the edge of the blinds, saw his Nissan parked close, the lot nearly empty. "God's mercy on me," he whispered, voice a rasp, then stood a little straighter, squared his shoulders, willed himself to get his bags from the Nissan, strip, shit, shower, shave, put himself together.

Renewed for another day, only a little shaky, cooled by the air conditioner, he puzzled out how to activate on high, he walked out, without a clue as to what to do, where to go beyond the need to move until he felt real enough to start thinking, planning.

And as he walked across the parking lot, his Nissan baking in the killer sun overhead now, a light sweat popping out on his face and neck, past the motel office he avoided for fear the geezers might still be at it, or a second shift of them, he improved rapidly.

Learst always liked walking—on trail in Nam, he never bitched— liked especially patrolling new ground. Marching through this blazing white-hot Arizona heat, cloudless sky, vegetation already starting to droop, he felt himself come back together, hangover fading to something like a terrible nightmare not remembered in detail. He remembered how good it felt the first days and weeks, months, elsewhere—Keweenaw Bay in the U.P., the high mesa outside Grand Junction, the low rolling treeless hills of north-central Oklahoma—the way things looked and felt good because they were new to him. Even Nam the first month or two of his tour. Even the Detroit neighborhoods he explored on foot and bike when he was a kid, a thousand years ago.

He passed The Blue Note, looking abandoned. What time did Skippy start his shift? He'd counted the bills in his wallet, groaned to see how much he'd dropped last night, but there was plenty to last until his disability reached him if he stayed put here a couple of weeks. Learst carried plenty of money, like a stash, when he cut and ran from wherever. To wherever.

And then he was passing the entrance to a trailer park, some geezer sitting under his trailer awning, a sign stuck in the fake grass mat as big as the awning, *Manager*. This geezer sat in a folding chair, a big orange juice in one hand. The geezer smiled at Learst like he'd been waiting for him, raised his orange juice, toasted him. Learst felt required to try something like a wave, a smile.

The geezer said, "You're looking pretty spry for a fellow put away his share and mine and who all else's as well!" He leaned forward in his chair, like Learst had come specifically to see him. This geezer wore plaid shorts, shower clogs, his legs and feet scrawny as sticks, but tanned. He wore a golfer's pullover, his hair a blond rug the color of his glass of orange juice. Learst figured he had to speak, walked up under the trailer awning, felt the contrasting cool of its shade.

Learst said, "I can't say I recall you from The Blue Note crowd. Fact, I can't recall much of any of it."

The geezer laughed, stood up, stuck out his hand; his fingers were bony, joints swollen, tanned arms as skinny as his legs. "Ed Jones," he said, and, "It's a common name but mine by birth all the same."

"Learst," Learst said. Ed Jones's hand felt cold in his. "I sort of overdid," he said.

"As long as you're paying for it in the morning, I call that a square deal, OK?" Ed Jones said. "It's when you wake with the heebie jeebies when you've not a drop taken that's your time to complain," he said.

"Then for sure I earned it I think," Learst said.

"What you're needing, young Mr. Learst," Ed Jones said, "is a touch of the grand elixir here." He raised his glass to Learst, sipped, smacked his lips, sighed. "I have an ancient secret formula. Grab that chair," he said, pointing with his glass at a folded chair leaning against his trailer. "I'll be back in a flash," he said, and dashed inside, the trailer's screen door slapping behind him.

Learst grabbed the chair, had trouble unfolding the aluminum legs, got it, set it down far enough away from Jones's to feel comfortable, sat down just as Jones kicked open his screen door, came out with a glass of orange juice as big as his own, handed it to Learst. There was a mush of crushed ice in it, the glass sharply cold in Learst's hand. "Sometimes I mix it with grapefruit juice for variety's sake," Ed Jones said. "Happy, happy," he said, toasted Learst again, drank. Learst took a small drink, then a long one. The vodka came through, a mild undercurrent.

"Lordy," Learst said.

"Oldest cure in the cosmos," Ed Jones said.

"I'll second the motion," Learst said, drank again. "So you caught my act last night, did you?" he said. He could feel the screwdriver melting the remains of his hangover, how good the awning's shade felt, a secure barrier against the boiling heat and razor light just a few feet away. He drank again.

"I'm to be found there most evenings," Ed Jones said. "They all but have a stool with my name on it."

"That Skippy's a good barkeep," Learst said.

"Skippy is one whale of a good guy," Ed Jones said. And he said, "So. You moving in or just passing on your way?" And Learst, loving the screwdriver's effects—Ed Jones got up to top him off twice—talked a deal more than he usually did.

"I'm not quite for certain," he said, and told Ed Jones the outlines, Nam, Upper Michigan, his disability, Grand Junction, Stillwater, Oklahoma, now here, on his way he didn't know where, or why exactly either. "Being frank," Learst said, "I seem to have become your legendary rolling stone."

Ed Jones, who told Learst he'd retired four years ago from college teaching—Milton his specialty—in Pennsylvania, said he'd been the same if only for a short while. "The wife and I, who happened to be my second such, by the way, parted ways. It happens in the best of families, I assure you," he said. "We have a daughter, who of course has her own life. She lives in Maryland, so I was pretty much at loose ends until I pulled stakes, sold off what I didn't want and the ex didn't get her mitts on, headed west, lit down here, and here I remain."

"I attempted that, staying put, three times now. I never got married officially, but I lived, you know, common law, with two women, one had a daughter also, a nice enough kid. This was just recent, Stillwater. I must be still looking for a spot to start over, best I understand it all, which I don't."

The secret, Ed Jones told him, was not looking back. "The trick's dumping all that, like the junk you sell at a yard sale, it's gone, you don't think on it, you pack your necessities and head on out, OK?"

"To where? What?" Learst said.

"Anywhere," Ed Jones said, and, "Here's as good as any. It's good for me. And a lot of other good folk I can introduce you to. The trick is," he said, "if you can junk the past, you don't need to fret the future." And Ed Jones went on to tell him about here, the outskirts of Tucson, Arizona,

the community of geezers—a word Learst knew better than to use—
he'd just by chance happened to land in in his Nissan pickup last night.

"You'll find we're not all cut from the same cloth here," Ed Jones said.
There were the golfers, he said. Just down the street, across the roads,
Whispering Pines was an example. Big houses, two cars in every attached garage, a clubhouse like a mansion, dining facilities, pro shop,
locker rooms with sauna, three nine-hole courses so one was always fallow. From the road you could see the sprinkler sprays keeping them
green as a garden, ornamental shrubs. "They're the money people," he
told Learst, "just a cut under the really big-money Sun City types, men
who cashed out their businesses or just clip coupons." They held golf
tournaments, competed for loving cups, threw big dances and costume
parties on all the holidays, rode their smooth-paved community streets
in fancy electric carts, children and grandchildren flying in for visits
from all over the country. "Very tony folk," Ed Jones said, and, "That's
not us here, OK?"

"It's for sure not me," Learst said, and they laughed.

"Then you got your codgers," Ed Jones said. "Silas and that sort, you'll
see some of them mixed right in with us here." He waved his hand at the
trailer park he managed.

"Retired lifers," Learst said.

"That, and just *old*," Ed Jones said. They didn't have the golfers'
money to be farting through silk. They sat around, played cards and
bingo and taught each other classes in foreign languages and the like at
a United Way Senior Center a few miles down the road. Went to doctors
at the drop of a hat. Some of them had pensions, at least Social Security—who didn't?—some of them, Ed Jones figured, got money in the
mail from their kids and grandkids, those who had any.

"How do you mean, *just old?*" Learst asked.

"I mean done living for all intents and purposes. Like Silas and his
cronies. Otis?" Ed Jones said. "All they talk about is their war stories,
their aches and pains, what pills they take how often, what they did for a
living back when, like it was any interest to anybody. Blink at them,
they'll haul out their photo albums, the old ladies," he said. And he said,
"That's not us, my gang, OK?"

Ed Jones's gang, he said, didn't have the golfers' money, but they weren't done living. They *lived,* he said. "I'll introduce you around. It's time the gang, some of them, will be gathering to eat a bite. The Pancake House, just a couple blocks down past your Desert Inn there, we usually mosey in about now for a late lunch before we hit poolside. You'll see," Ed Jones said. "We live life like we enjoy life is how I'd put it."

"The Blue Note," Learst said.

"That's a good instance of it," Ed Jones said. "What it comes to is, it's *now,*" he said.

"Now," Learst said.

"Put away your drink there, " Ed Jones said. "I'd offer you another, but I don't like to see a man get warped when there's a whole new day and night ahead of him yet."

"I don't make it a habit getting blitzed before it's dark," Learst said.

"Give me your glass," Ed Jones said. "We'll take us a stroll. I want you to meet the gang. You'll like the Pancake House," he said.

It was like walking through a furnace, down past The Blue Note, the Desert Inn, to the Pancake House. Learst felt his skin pop a thick sweat-film. He thought of the chill summers in the U.P. in the Keweenaw Invisible Army, the high, thin cold air of the big mesa at Grand Junction, the humid summers of northern Oklahoma. "It does get warm," he said.

Ed Jones said, "You get used to it to where you scarcely notice."

The Pancake House felt like the inside of a refrigerator, Learst momentarily blinded as he passed out of the direct sunlight into the air-conditioning. Ed Jones's gang sat at a big corner horseshoe booth, drinking iced tea and coffee, smoking cigarettes all around. Pancake House was crowded.

"The last man out the door!" Skippy said, smiling big, and, "A survivor if I ever saw one!" There was laughter, and Ed Jones introduced him to the gang—there were others, not there, he said, but these were the faithful. Learst leaned over the table to shake their tanned hands, leathery to his touch.

There was Skippy, and a very tall skinny man in a haltertop exposing a lot of grizzled chest hair who half-stood, introduced as Decker; a short, fat, and totally bald geezer, his skull tanned and freckled like the rest of him, called Dale; and three women, Linda, Lizzie, and Randi. Randi was nearly as tall as Learst, the only one not tanned near brown.

Her skin was reddish, sun-broiled. The women all wore shorts, lots of jewelry and makeup, bra-less under their skimpy blouses. Learst tried not to look at their shrunken, dropping breasts.

"So," Skippy said to Ed Jones, "did you have to revive him wherever it was you stumbled on him?"

"I gave him," Ed Jones said, "a small taste of a restorative." The gang all thought that was very funny.

"Pacing is everything," Decker said. He wore thick glasses and a gold ID bracelet that slid up and down his hairy arm.

"I saw you going after it with both hands," Lizzie said. "You better put a limit on him tonight, Skippy," she said.

Dale said, "Are you a new neighbor?"

"He's at Desert Inn," Ed Jones said.

"Those old farts," Randi said.

Linda said, "You better talk to Ed, he can give you a break on one of his vacant double-wides if you ask nice." And all the gang laughed some more.

A waitress they all knew—her name was Winnie, as old as any of the gang—took their orders. Learst watched them order off the lite-calorie menu, choose senior discounts. He opted for black coffee only.

"No vitamins in that juice," Lizzie said.

Dale said, "You need your proteins to get through a day with this crew."

Decker said, "My weight's constant no matter what I eat no matter how much." Linda and Randi told him he had no cause to complain; men's metabolism was a breeze compared to a woman's. They talked a lot about their food, how their weight was constant, how good their blood pressure was, how they never felt better, how they looked forward to a pool dip and lying out in this wonderful sun after they ate.

Learst scoped the Pancake House, sipped his coffee. Ed Jones was right, had them pegged; they weren't all alike. At tables beyond the counter, in far booths, as if roped off from the gang and the counter, were what had to be the golfers. They were mostly couples, better dressed, softer spoken, lots of gray and blue-rinsed white hair, eating and drinking as if the gang and the counter weren't there. The counter stool crowd was mostly solitaries, mute. They ate slowly, mechanically, as if by the numbers, some of them glued to newspapers, some just staring straight ahead like they saw nothing, their faces half-angry, half-bored. The golfers and the codgers, Learst thought. And the gang, talking loud, laughing, the way teenagers acted up in restaurants.

Finished eating, the gang all lit more cigarettes. Learst had never seen so many old people smoking together like that. Skippy lit his Camel for him with his butane lighter. "Me for the pool," Lizzie said after her third cigarette. The ashtray held filter-tips smeared with lipstick. Learst kept waiting for them to ask him questions, for an opening to ask them about themselves. Where did everyone come from? Except for maybe the weather, why here?

"Me right on you tail, lady!" Dale said.

"I love it when he talks dirty!" Randi said, and the gang whooped at that one.

"Join us, a dip'll set you straight," Skippy said. Learst figured why not.

There were more of Ed Jones's gang at the in-ground pool set in a sort of court area, cracked tiles and cement, surrounded by the trailers he managed. He and Skippy took him around, introduced Learst to the geezers, men and women lying out on colorful beach towels at the edge of the water that glittered like steel shards in the sweltering sun, stinking of chlorine. Learst, awash with sweat, knelt and leaned over to shake hands, then followed them from poolside to the blessed shade of a cabana roof and a few tables with umbrellas where more geezers sat. Almost all of them hid their eyes behind reflecting sunglasses, their bodies slick with coconut-smelling oils and lotions. "Learst," he said when he was introduced, and, "I think I'm just passing through." He looked away from the half-dozen long surgical scars exposed by two-piece swimsuits and spandex trunks.

There was an Eddie, missing an arm, his stump puckered just below his shoulder, his other arm tattooed with a large butterfly, a Tillie, who looked eighty if she was a day, sagging out of a yellow bikini, a Morty exercising with dumbbells under the cabana, a Charlie who seemed to be trying to see if he could outsqueeze Learst with his grip, a Sandy who took Learst's hand in both of hers, a Dot who lay on her stomach with her bathing suit top untied, clasped it to her oversize chest with one hand while she shook Learst's with the other, a Marty, a Buddy, a Flossie, a Denny—their names fluttered in Learst's head. He held his breath against the smells of sunblockers and tanning creams, pool chlorine, the odor of heated flesh.

A boombox played old-fashioned music Learst didn't recognize from the cabana, and every few minutes a geezer got up, padded barefoot to buy a soda from a machine that clunked hard when it spit out the can. They said things like, "You making it OK?" and, "Grab a suit and get yourself wet," and, "Welcome to the club," and, "Didn't I see you at The Blue Note last night?" to which a woman who looked a little like Learst remembered his mother said, "Fresh meat!"

They lay, tanning, baking, talked softly to each other, drank sodas, oiled themselves and each other, listened to the boombox music, smoked cigarettes. It was like a kids' beach party without sand or dancing or cooking out, like, Learst thought, a lot of dying, half-dead bodies who looked good for their ages, laid out for tagging whenever somebody got around to it.

"This heat's a killer," he said to Ed Jones and Skippy.

"Strip off, catch the rays," Skippy said, already down to the trunks he wore under his slacks.

"Hit the water," Ed Jones said, stepping out of his walking shorts, his trunks a tartan plaid. "I can fetch you a suit from my trailer."

"Maybe another time," Learst said, because no one used the pool. He stood in the shade, tried to think of the cold in Upper Michigan, on the mesa at Grand Junction, but all that came to him were flashes of the humid Oklahoma summers, the bush heat and wet that rotted his battle dress as he walked trail in Nam. He wanted to blank his mind, scoped the greasy geezer bodies glistening in the sun, the women's painted toe-nails and fingernails, the boombox music, the whirr of trailer air conditioners, the spikes of TV antennas like the ribbing for a huge dome over them that didn't keep out heat or blinding light.

"So," Skippy said. "The gang, right?"

"Most of them," Ed Jones said.

Learst said, "I think I need to get to my room, shower, maybe crash a while."

"Whatever suits," Skippy said.

"Will you grace us for Sundowners?" Ed Jones asked.

"What?"

"Happy Hour," Skippy said, and, "Two for one, Double Bubble we call it. The Blue Note. I go in at four, the gang'll all be there."

"Most of them," Ed Jones said.

"Most probably," Learst said, shook hands with them.

"Think on sticking around a while, we can always use new blood," Ed Jones said. "I do have a vacant double-wide I can shoot you a deal on, week to week if you don't want to sign a lease right off, OK?"

"I'll think on it," Learst said, left them to trek through the suffocating heat to his motel. He was going to shower, he promised himself, maybe get a decent meal at that Pancake House, get in his Nissan as soon as the sun went down, move on, west, south. Anywhere. This was no place for him to try staying put even for a little while.

Back in his room, Learst, sodden, legs unsteady, head thick from the sun, eyes bleared, was certain he'd hit the road that night. But a long shower, first hot, then gradually colder until he felt chilled to the bone, followed by a deep sleep without dreams, made him feel better, confident. Dressed in clean jeans and a sport shirt, he meant to pay up and check out when he went to the Desert Inn office, but the air, many degrees cooler with a light breeze stirring the darkness, put a spring in his step as he crossed the asphalt lot past his Nissan. He was surprised to find Silas alone in the office, watching television with the sound on this time. "How do?" Silas said. "You recovered any?"

"Where's your pals?" Learst said, fingered his room key in his pocket.

"They'll be by in time," Silas said. "Something?" he asked.

Learst surprised himself when he said, "I just stopped in to say hi."

"Where you off to this night, or shouldn't I ask?" Silas said.

"I thought I might catch The Blue Note's Double Bubble if it's not too late," he said, surprised he said that.

"That bunch," Silas said, shook his head like Learst had said something shameful.

"You know them? Skippy? Ed Jones?"

"Everybody knows everybody. Act like stupid kids," Silas said.

"They're OK," Learst said, as if defending himself.

"What's a youngster like you hanging out with that crazy outfit?"

"I just met them last night and today," Learst said, and, "Crazy in what way?"

"What kind of life is that, boozing and sitting out frying by their pool in the sun, jumping in and out of each other's beds from what I hear," Silas said, clucked his tongue.

"Is that what they do?" Learst said.

"Losers," Silas said, looked back at his television.

"How's that?"

"What else you call a bunch of doddering old men and ladies too living out their lives like that? One or another of them's always getting hair transplants and their busts expanded and the like I hear."

"Maybe I'm just as much of a loser," Learst said. Silas turned to him.

"So what's your story?" he said, and, "You were saying you served in Vietnam if I remember right?"

"I did," Learst said. And then he said more he had not at all meant to. He said, "And then I was back in Detroit where I was raised after I separated at Fort Hood, Texas, where all I did was blitz myself regularly, in Detroit, and mooched off my old man who's a widower until he threw me out, and tried to kick some habits I picked up in Nam."

"You one of them dopeheads, are you?" Silas said.

"I was until I kicked it," he said. He said, "Then I moved up to the U.P. You ever heard of the Keweenaw Peninsula? Keweenaw Bay?" Silas shook his head. "A lot of us from Nam, guys from Michigan and other places also, we congregated up there. We had a regular firebase camp in the woods, nothing but Indians living anywhere near. We even had a name. We called ourselves the Keweenaw Invisible Army. K.I.A. Get it?"

"I get it," Silas said, and, "So you're one of these post-trauma soldiers I hear about, are you?"

"I was. Long enough to get disability out of it. Then I left the U.P. I went to Colorado." Don't bother telling this, Learst thought.

"Why leave when you got it made in the shade with your buddies?" Silas said.

"It wasn't going anywhere. There wasn't a future there," he said.

"There ain't any here either," Silas said. They were silent a moment.

Then he said, "Not with that bunch of losers. They got about as much *future* as me," he said.

"So what *do* you got?" Learst said. He did not want to know.

"Thirty years honorable service, and this here job which allows me free residence, which allows me to do things for my kids. I got three kids, one of which is also career military in the Air Force, and I had a wife I married in Japan, Japanese woman, until she died with cancer of the breast. And I also got friends who you met if you weren't so schnockered you don't remember them."

"Otis and Merle," Learst said.

"Merle and Otis," Silas said, "who also got honorable military service careers of thirty years each."

"What's that besides war stories?" Learst said. Silas got a look on his face like he was going to get up and come at him. But he didn't, stayed sitting, turned back to the television.

"You call it what you like," he said, and, "It's mine and it's honorable, and it's better than your Blue Note crazies playing like they're still kids until they drop in their tracks, which happens every so often, by the way."

"I didn't mean an insult," Learst said.

"I didn't say it was," Silas said. "You're too young to know what I'm talking about. Go get yourself a snootful with your Blue Note comrades."

"Maybe I will if it looks like a good thing," Learst said, and left. He shuddered as he walked down the dark street to The Blue Note, as if the cooling air was colder than inside Silas's office. He shuddered and put Silas and his geezer lifer pals out of his mind, shook himself to put away thinking about the U.P., the K.I.A., to stop thinking the word *future*.

"Am I too late for your Double Bubble?" Learst asked Skippy.

"Only a tad," Skippy said, "but I make exceptions for friends, right?" and, "You planning on drowning yourself again?" he said as he poured Learst a double vodka rocks, set it on a napkin for him, slid an ashtray closer to him on the bar.

"I think I'll just puddle jump a little tonight," he said, took a light from the bartender. "Crowd's smaller," he said, swiveling his captain's chair stool to scope The Blue Note.

"So so," Skippy said. "Menu?" The bartender looked good in his red vest and black sleeve garters, frilly shirt, white tinged bluish by the recessed lighting.

"Maybe later," Learst said. He nursed his drink, checked out the crowd that grew a little as he watched, geezers coming in in pairs like they were on heavy dates, taking tables in corners away from the bar. He recognized some of them from the pool, lifted his glass when they waved and winked at him. And he watched singles at the bar, getting up to pair off with singles at tables, listened to the old-fashioned music coming from somewhere, watched the first couples get up to slow dance.

"It's nice in here," he said to Skippy when he pushed his glass toward him for a refill.

"It's always nice here," Skippy said. "This is a great place. I wouldn't trade it for anywhere," he said.

"I can see why," Learst said. His drinks gave him a feeling that everything was pretty much right, he wasn't worried about taking off in any hurry, didn't feel like thinking about where he might be headed this time. When Ed Jones came in, all spiffed up in a sports coat, creased slacks, shoes with brass buckles on them, Learst waved him to join him at the bar.

"Now how'd I know you'd show?" Ed Jones said, took the stool next to him.

"Have one on me," Learst said, gestured Skippy over. "Build this man one on my tab," he said, and bought one for the bartender also. The music sounded louder as they talked, more couples dancing close and slow.

"I love nights like this," Ed Jones said, and, "Does it get any better?" Skippy said, "Not in my book."

"Is this all you people do?" Learst couldn't stop himself from asking.

"All what?" Ed Jones said.

"This," Learst said. "Hang out here, eat at Pancake House, lay out at that pool of yours?"

"There supposed to be more?" Skippy said, laughed, slapped the bar, went away to take a drink order from the waitress too old for the outfit she wore.

"We do whatever suits us," Ed Jones said. He swiveled his stool to face Learst directly. He said, "If we feel like boozing it, we booze it. We get the urge for a dip, we hit the pool. Catch rays? We catch rays. Food's good at the Pancake House, cheap besides, we eat when we're hungry."

"Nobody works?" Learst said.

"I work. I manage the court, which gives me my double-wide free. Skippy works. I think he works more for the fun of talking to people than the money. Oh," he said, "people have their various interests. I know one gal's a great reader, she gets a sack of books every week at the library branch. Another one, she's loyal to her soap, wouldn't miss it for the life of her. Some people have their hobbies," he said.

"I noticed nobody's married seems like," Learst said.

"There's a few. Everyone I know's been there, most more than once or twice even," Ed Jones said. "Plenty got grown kids, but it's not like your golfers, families coming down on you every long weekend."

"Sounds like it could get boring," Learst said.

"Never a dull moment with this gang," Ed Jones said, and, "We have a lot of laughs." They heard Skippy laughing loud with customers down the bar.

"I guess if you like it," Learst said.

"It's what's now is what it is," Ed Jones said.

Learst had another round, then another, wasn't sure if Skippy was still pouring him doubles or not. Ed Jones went away to talk with a couple at one of the tables, came back, went away again, came back. Learst had no idea what time it was until he noticed some of the couples heading out, yelling goodnight to Skippy. Learst knew he was at least partially blitzed—he never ordered any food—when he started telling Ed Jones and Skippy about where he'd been before this. It was one of the few times he could think of when he wanted to talk about it.

He said, "Did you guys know I'm pushing fifty? I never dreamed I'd be fifty, you know, when I was a kid?" Ed Jones and Skippy laughed, said he didn't look it, fifty was no age at all. They invited Learst to guess their ages, but he had more he wanted to say.

"I think about it," he said, "and what did I ever accomplish? The thing of it is, I never got on any kind of a track to anywhere. It's like, I was a kid, your average kid in Detroit, I probably'd tried to get on with Ford in the plant, like my dad, but the draft got me for Nam, which kind of swerved me off the track."

"Is this a war story?" Ed Jones said. He and Skippy smiled at him.

"Not a scratch," Learst said. "I mean, I was a grunt, 101st, except I wasn't a paratroop. I know some guys got hurt and killed, but I never so much as stubbed my toe." He was lucky, a charmed life, they said.

"I did get to using weed some, but not serious," Learst said, and, "I started using fairly serious when I got back to Fort Hood, and when I went back to Michigan I kind of just laid out until the old man got married again to this bitch and asked me polite to move on." They nodded their heads at him like it had happened the same way to them.

"Then I hooked up with this one crazy, Dan Mix, I knew in Nam, we lived like only blocks away from each other and we first meet in Nam, right? So I hook up with him and we go up to the U.P. to sort of like start all over clean, see?" They nodded. "You know where Keweenaw Bay is? Really, it was a lot of dropouts from Nam gathered up to live like we were still there. We lived in tents, we went hunting out of season illegally, which is where I got to using more weed and some other shit, which I saw was going nowhere. By this time I'm all strung out, so I went to the V.A., which gave me my disability I been living on since."

"That's a sad story," Skippy said.

Ed Jones said, "Aren't they all?"

Then Learst told them about Colorado, the big mesa at Grand Junction, the woman he lived with. "She was an all-right woman, but I couldn't see us going anywhere, she wasn't very interested in permanent, so ultimately after some years I split and went to Oklahoma, just on a whim." He was going to tell them about Oklahoma, the woman there with the daughter he could have adopted if he'd been willing to get married, but didn't get the chance.

Ed Jones said, "Why carry all that baggage?"

Skippy said, "Ed's right. You're not some golfer's got coupons to clip with family visiting you every vacation like nothing's changed in life, right?"

Ed Jones said, "You don't want to be like those deadheads playing cards and bird-watching in the desert while they wait around to croak."

Skippy said, "You think our gang doesn't have sad stories to tell if we didn't know that's a waste of time? You see any of us chewing the fat about what was, like old Silas and Merle? Otis?"

Ed Jones said, "Chuck it why don't you? You got your health, you got your military service pension, well deserved, enjoy it, OK?"

Learst was about to tell them he felt like he had to get somewhere, get started on something, make a plan for the future—he was pushing god-damn fifty, had to get something going. But Skippy went down the bar to light some lady geezer's cigarette, and Ed Jones said he had to drain his lizard, walked off into the bluish dimness to the men's. Learst was going to have maybe one more drink, go to his motel and sleep on it, hope he'd see things clear in the morning, but when he was about to sig-nal Skippy for a refill, the geezer gal came up from one of the tables and asked him to dance.

"Dance with the lady?" she said.

"Me?" Learst said. She looked pretty good in the blue lighting, tanned gold-brown, bleached blonde, big chest, goodish legs, a lot of bracelets that clinked when she moved her arms. He almost got off his stool. "I'm not much of a dancer except for the two-step I learned a while back," he said.

"I'll lead, you just follow," she said, and, "I met you at the pool. Obviously I didn't make a first impression, huh?"

"No," he said. "I mean, I recognize you, but I'm no good on names."

"I'll whisper mine in your ear while we waltz," she said.

"Give a rain check," Learst said. "I'm not exactly steady on my pins," he said, held up his empty glass to her.

She reached out, bracelets clinking, patted his cheek, laughed, said, "It's a date," went back to her table where he heard her laughing with her geezer gal friends. Skippy came up to pour him a fresh one.

"Don't tell me you turned that away," he said, winked, smiled big.

"I'll grant you she looks pretty good for her age," Learst said.

"A little silicon here," Skippy said, "a little tuck there, a little liposuc-tion if needed," he said, slapped the bartop. "Like my facial hair," he said.

"With me she's cradle robbing," Learst said.

"All cats in the dark, they say," Skippy said. Learst was about to ask her name when Ed Jones returned from the lavatory. "I think somebody just tried to pick up my man here," the bartender said.

"What are you, hard to get?" Ed Jones said. He said, "Me too. Now Skippy here, he's in a permanent state of hot to trot." He and Skippy laughed hard.

Then Learst said, "Ed, about that double-wide without a lease?"

"My door's always open," the trailer park manager said.

"What it is," Learst said, "I need to get an address so they can forward my disability from Stillwater."

"Stay as long as you like, no sweat," Ed Jones said.

"Who knows," Skippy said, "give it time, she may ask you again when you're in a better mood, right?" They all three laughed at that. Learst finished his last drink, waved back when the pretty good-looking geezer gal waved at him on her way out with her friends.

It wasn't, he thought, like he was going to stay any longer than he needed to think things through.

Learst liked his double-wide. Less than two blocks around a corner from Ed Jones's, two blocks the other way from the pool, it was the most living space he'd had since leaving his dad's house in Detroit. He had two bedrooms, a living room with a big console TV, a good-size kitchen, full bath, storage space up the kazoo. It still felt near empty after he moved his things in from his Nissan, but he didn't spend all that much time there anyhow.

There was an aluminum awning if he felt like sitting outside in the late mornings, a covered space to park the Nissan out of the blistering sun, and with the window blinds down to cut off the glare, the roof air conditioner kept it even cooler than Learst liked. Sometimes he spent an afternoon inside, lights off, cold air chugging in, the TV on—it was like a bunker, a perfect cold, dry place out of the desert heat and dust, nothing could touch him.

When he checked out of his motel, Silas said, "That's a shame, man only your age joining up with those old crazies."

Learst told him, "It's only until my disability gets to me, I don't have a lease." Silas clucked his tongue, shook his head like he'd heard bad news. What the hell, Learst thought, did that old lifer know about anything except his war stories?

And he liked the days as they passed. Some mornings he sat out under his awning, sometimes poured himself a hair off the dog if he'd overdone it the night before, kicked back until some of the gang walked by on their way to the Pancake House for brunch, joined them. Some mornings he walked down to Ed Jones's or Skippy's trailer, where he was usually offered a pop or two, went off with them to brunch. If the word was out that Skippy had a woman staying overnight, Learst knew to stay away, meet up with him later at the pool.

He liked brunch at the Pancake House. He got to eating the soup and salad special. Ed Jones showed him how to dip the ladle deep into the soup cauldron to bring up the thick vegetables, and he imitated the way Skippy heaped a salad plate with cottage cheese and garbanzos for maximum mass and weight and protein. He liked sitting with whoever of the gang was there in their corner booth, smoking, drinking coffee and iced tea, talking about whatever—nobody asked personal questions, he never mentioned the U.P. or Colorado or Oklahoma or Nam, never asked anyone how many times they were married, if they had children, where they came from, what they once worked at.

He liked sitting over coffee refills, smoking, scoping the customers at tables, at the counter, golfer-types in their expensive-looking clothes, their good manners, the old coots at the counter like zombies, noses buried in newspapers or scowling at nothing in the middle of the air. He liked laughing at little things with the gang, smiling a lot, nobody crabby or sour-assed about anything, like none of them had any troubles ever to stew about.

And he liked the pool. He cut off a pair of old jeans for a swimsuit, wore them like shorts to the Pancake House, hopped in the water for a quick dip, lay on a towel on the concrete to dry off in seconds. In the full-length mirror in his double-wide's bathroom, he checked out the faint tan lines at his waist and thighs, ankles.

Just once, sitting next to Ed Jones under the cabana roof, he said, "You know I was meaning to tell you about what happened with me in Oklahoma, this woman with a daughter I could have got married to if I wanted. Why I didn't and all."

"Don't," Ed Jones said. And he said, "You don't really want to rake that over any more than I want to show you my skeletons, OK?"

"I guess," Learst said, decided Ed Jones was right, what was the point?

In less than two weeks after he moved in, he got his mail forwarded from Stillwater, his disability check.

And he liked nights at The Blue Note. He never missed Double Bubble, but never let himself get more than half-blitzed, didn't always close the place either. He took to dressing a little for his nights, clean sport shirt, pressed slacks, shined his one pair of good shoes, shaved, used a dab of gel on his hair.

"You know," Learst said after Skippy lit his cigarette for him, "sometimes I think I could sit here like this forever."

"Is that you," Skippy said, grinning, "or the potato juice talking?"

"Some of both," Learst said.

He liked getting semi-blitzed, liked to watch the dancers—some of them pretty good at it—liked watching to see who paired off with whom, or which couple stopped being a couple, no longer danced close or nuzzled off in a corner, couples who wouldn't be lying out side-by-side to get their rays the next day at the pool.

"This reminds me," he said to Ed Jones, "of the way kids in my high school used to date, going steady, breaking up, then steadies again."

"Hey," Ed Jones said, "the eternal nature of the beast, OK? What are you, keeping track?" He wasn't, just found it interesting, fun to observe.

One night, slightly more than half-blitzed, the pretty good-looking one who asked him to dance—her name was Dot—did it again. This time he got up, tried following her, then tried to teach her the two-step. He had half a notion to ask her how old she was, but didn't. Back at the bar, he had the waitress take her a drink on him, and she toasted him from across the room with it, waved her arm, rattling her bracelets.

"I do believe she fancies you," Skippy said.

"I'm half-tempted," Learst said.

"You wouldn't be sorry," the bartender said, and, "I speak from experience."

"Maybe some other time," he said.

"No time like the present, right?" Skippy said.

What he liked in these days after moving in was he almost never caught himself thinking about anything serious. He didn't think about Nam, or Keweenaw Bay, or the big mesa, or Oklahoma. He caught himself thinking he wasn't thinking about where he was headed next. Relax, Learst told himself. What's the rush? What's the point? Enjoy it while it lasts, he told himself. And he did.

Then Skippy died.

Learst, off in his Nissan to buy groceries and get a haircut, didn't find out until he got to The Blue Note, just in time for Double Bubble. The crowd was about the usual, Ed Jones on his regular swivel-stool, but the bartender wasn't Skippy. This bartender was a larger man Learst didn't know, maybe a little younger than Skippy. He wore a short-sleeve shirt that showed his very muscular arms for a guy his age, his hair, as white as Skippy's, cut crew-style, like a college kid. He was at the other end of the bar when Learst took his place beside Ed Jones.

"Where you been?" Ed Jones said.

"I had some shopping," Learst said, and he said, "What's with this? Where's Skippy?" he said, nodding toward the new bartender with muscled arms and crew-cut hair.

"That's Matt," Ed Jones said, and, "He's tended before for Skippy's vacations days, subbing."

"Skippy's on vacation?" Learst said.

Ed Jones said, "Skippy's left us." The new bartender came down to take Learst's order.

He said, "Hi. Matt's the name," held out a big tanned hand, shook Learst's. Learst told him vodka rocks, saw he checked the backbar clock to see if it was still Double Bubble before he poured the drink. He didn't give him a napkin or push an ashtray close to him, asked if he wanted to run a tab, left when Learst told him yes. This bartender looked to Ed Jones, who nodded his head yes, vouched for Learst.

"He afraid I'd stiff him?" Learst asked.

"He didn't know you is all, now he does, OK?" Ed Jones said.

"So where'd Skippy go for his vacation?" Learst said. "He never mentioned it to me."

"I said," Ed Jones said, "*left* us. Passed. Passed away," he said. It felt to Learst like he didn't speak for several minutes. Ed Jones sipped at his drink. Learst took out a cigarette, caught himself waiting for Skippy to zip down the bar with his butane lighter. He put the Camel back in the pack, looked at his drink but didn't taste it. He scoped The Blue Note.

The crowd was about normal. There was Dot, the dancer, at a table with a couple of lady friends, giggling, smoking, putting drinks away. At another table sat Decker and Linda, who, the story was, were currently an item. They were side by side at their table, semi-nuzzling. There was Randi, slow-dancing in a far corner with Buddy. There was Lizzie, not far down the bar, leaning on the bar to talk with Matt, this new bartender, who covered one of her hands with his. Learst tasted his drink, wet his mouth with cold vodka to be sure he could speak.

He said, "What the hell," and, "Tell me about this, Ed." Ed Jones spoke out of the corner of his mouth, not looking at him.

"In his sleep, it looks like," he said. "He wasn't at brunch, you may have noticed, but that's nothing so strange. He wasn't at the pool, which is also not that odd. Neither were you, OK? When he didn't come in for his shift here, Polly"—Polly was the waitress—"called but got no answer. He didn't have a machine. So she rang me. I walked over to his trailer. When I couldn't raise him I went and got my passkey. He was in bed, like he was sleeping, eyes closed and all, cold to the touch. I called 911, he's gone. You could have passed the ambulance on your way out here for all I know. So he's gone," Ed Jones said.

Learst said, "It doesn't look to have put any damper on the party, does it," and swiveled to scan the room. The music, like always, played from somewhere, the blue light the same as ever.

Ed Jones said, "It happens. Why should it?"

"He was a friend," Learst said.

"Certainly he was," Ed Jones said, and, "Are we supposed to drag out the crepe and tear our hair out? Life goes on, OK?" he said.

"Jesus," Learst said. He said, "When's the funeral or memorial or whatever?" He tried his drink again, but it had no taste.

Ed Jones said, "I haven't the foggiest."

"Has he got people to be informed?" Learst said.

Ed Jones turned to him now, looked him in the eyes for a beat, then said, "Drop it, will you, Learst?"

"You all," Learst said, "must either be pretty damn tough or cold-hearted to the max."

Ed Jones spoke louder now, as if he meant the crowd to hear. "Think about it!" he said. "You like us to all sit out by the pool with candles, get somebody to say a eulogy, what a great guy he was? We already know that, OK? You want organ music, flowers, rent a big church like the golfers do when one of their bunch kicks off and the relatives zoom in for the inheritance money? You want all the gals here he shagged sobbing so their makeup runs down their face? You want us drawing lots to see who's pall bearers? Or we could sit around here with a jug and tell stories about him back when, like Silas and his chums. You want that? Maybe we should put a sign up in the Pancake House, name our booth after him? Hey, Skippy was here, now he's not. Drink up, it's Double Bubble another four minutes by my watch. I'll buy."

Matt the new bartender came down to check on them, refilled Ed Jones, looked at Learst's still-full glass, looked at him like he wondered if Learst belonged. Learst shook his head no, laid money on the bar.

He said to Ed Jones, "This ain't my way, I guess. Christ, I'd do more for a pet dog if I had one died."

"Skippy," Ed Jones said, "is not the first one in our gang to leave us, he won't be the last. If you feel you have to honor his memory or something," he said, "live like he was still with us. That's our way," he said.

"I think I have to go," Learst said.

"Do what pleases and feels good, my motto," Ed Jones said, got up, took his drink from the bar, went over to Dot's table. She looked up, motioned Learst to come over. He waved like he didn't understand, got up and left.

Learst spent a day and a half inside his double-wide. He fixed a couple of meals for himself, watched a little television, took his sleep in short naps sometimes sitting up in front of the TV. Most of the time— he wasn't sure how many actual hours—he lay on his bed, lights out, shades down, blinds shut, no sound but the whir and chatter of his roof air conditioner. He could tell day from night by the slits of white sunlight at the bedroom's single window, but had no clock to give him the exact time. Learst lay on the bed, didn't undress, hands locked behind his head on the pillow, thinking.

He thought about Skippy, how it was wrong to let a man die, disappear, with no funeral, no burial, as if he'd walked off into the desert without telling anyone. It was wrong, Learst thought, to just go on living as if Skippy never was, never lived, tended the Blue Note bar and ate brunches at the Pancake House, hung out at the pool, chased after geezer-gal tail.

But the more he thought about this, Skippy, the harder it got for him to remember him clearly, exactly. Learst worked at it, brought up Skippy's snowy, swirled hairdo, dyed black eyebrows and small beard, red vest, sleeve garters, butane lighter, perfect capped teeth, big smile, rapping the bartop, the way he always said *right?* after he said something . . . but the harder Learst worked at this, *seeing* Skippy, the fuzzier and thinner all the details got. Thinking, Learst decided, about Skippy made the bartender all the less real. So what was the point?

He tried thinking about himself, about himself a kid in Detroit, about Nam, about himself in the Keweenaw Invisible Army with Dan Mix, but all that was also fuzzy and thin, years gone, dead as Skippy was.

He thought about Colorado, Grand Junction, the big mesa, the woman there, but this was no better, no more clear, hard memories than he had of Skippy. Thinking about Stillwater, Oklahoma, there was maybe a little more to it, that woman, her little daughter he could have adopted if he wanted, but there wasn't all that much, and there was nothing to think about once he got to the part where he broke with the woman, packed up, moved out, moved on. He remembered that woman teaching him the two-step in the cowboy bar they liked, but this made him think of Dot and her bracelets and big silicon tits, trying to teach her the two-step, her trying to teach him to slow-dance, and this embarrassed him, so he quit thinking, trying to think about any of all that. What was the point?

And when he focused on what to do next, now, nothing at all came to him, no California or Mexico or anywhere, anything, so it came back to him, Learst, there in the very dark, very chilly air-conditioned bedroom in a double-wide parked in a trailer court on the edge of Tucson proper, stretched out in his clothes, once in a while slipping in and out of near sleep during which his dreams, if any, were too small, short, confused.

For a while, maybe an hour or two at the end, that seemed OK, Learst alone in the dark and almost-cold, the noisy air conditioner like a kind of music, nothing and nobody except himself, not thinking about anything anywhere.

A day and a half passed, it was mid-morning, and Learst pulled himself up, grabbed a shower, shaved, found his cut-off jeans and his sneakers, a T-shirt, went out. The sun hit him like a hammer, but he squinted against it, walked, a little shaky on his feet from lying down so long, to Ed Jones's trailer-office.

And Ed Jones was there, under his awning for the shade, his orange-vodka drink matching the color of his bad hairpiece, smiling at him when Learst joined him in the shade. Ed Jones said, "I'd like to thought you'd gone off on us if it wasn't for your truck still there whenever I checked."

"I kind of crashed for a while," Learst said, and, "You going to Pancake House to eat?"

"Indeed," Ed Jones said, and, "Decker and Randi and some others are coming by shortly. You're welcome," he said.

"I could use somebody else's cooking," Learst said. He stood in the awning's shade, squinted down the asphalt street for a sign of any of the gang coming to go to brunch. "What I was thinking," he said, "was about a lease on my place there." He waited for Ed Jones to say something. When he didn't, Learst said, "Maybe I could see my way to taking a short one, three months. Six?"

Ed Jones said, "I imagine I could cut it to fit," and, "What say I fix you a small picker-upper to whet your appetite, we'll go get some brunch with the gang, come back here and I'll get the paper going, OK?"

"Sounds good," Learst said. And it did. He looked down the street, saw three of the gang coming their way. He was hungry, ready for a good feed. After he signed his lease, he figured to lay out at the pool for a bit, hang out, hit The Blue Note for Double Bubble. Ed Jones came out with a drink for him. Learst took a sip, tasted the spark of the vodka in it, sighed.

Learst looked out over the trailers, into the burned desert stretching away from him. No way, he thought, he was ever going to get himself up early in the mornings, before the sun became a furnace, to go exploring, walk into the desert. He had no interest in walking new ground, the way he once did, always enjoyed.

"Here's to today, and the next one to come, and the one after if need be," Ed Jones said, clinked his glass against Learst's.

"With you on that," Learst said, and said, "Happy, happy," and drank deep.

Acknowledgments

These stories, since revised, appeared
originally in the following journals:

"Looking for the Lost Eden," *The Chariton Review;* "A Dialogue," *New Orleans Review;* "The White Elephant," *The Chariton Review;* "Dirt," *Sandlapper;* "And What Should I Do in Illyria?" *High Plains Literary Review;* "Elder's Revenge," *Louisiana Literature;* "Learst's Last Stand," *The Long Story.* "Psychic Friends" is reprinted from *Shenandoah: The Washington and Lee University Review,* with the permission of the editor.

About the Author

Gordon Weaver, Professor Emeritus of English at Oklahoma State University, lives in Cedarburg, Wisconsin. He is the author of numerous books, including *Four Decades* and *Long Odds,* both available from the University of Missouri Press.

Photo by Leslie Jost